CURSE OF YAKSHINI

RAHUL CHATTERJEE

Dear Readers,

As I conclude the journey of *Yakshini*, I want to extend my heartfelt gratitude to each of you for embarking on this adventure with me. This story is more than just a tale of supernatural forces and ancient mysteries; it is a reflection of the deep-rooted cultural legends that make India such a remarkable land.

India is a country rich in history, mythology, and timeless tales that have shaped our identity over millennia. I have always felt a profound connection to these stories and a strong desire to share them with the world. The cultural heritage of India is vast, and I believe that the world needs to know about the legends and narratives that have been an integral part of our existence.

Before writing *Yakshini*, I authored another book titled *Samaykaal*, which explored the fascinating concept of time travel and served as a tribute to our great Sanatan Dharma. Both these books stem from my deep respect for the traditions and beliefs that have been passed down through generations in our country. Through my work, I aim to bring these stories to a wider audience, showcasing the richness and diversity of India's cultural tapestry.

As a filmmaker and editor by profession, storytelling is my passion. Whether through the lens of a camera or the pages of a book, my goal has always been to create narratives that resonate with the human spirit and connect us to our roots.

Thank you for allowing me to share this story with you. I
hope that *Yakshini* has not only entertained you but also
offered a glimpse into the mystical and enchanting world
of Indian folklore.

With gratitude,

Rahul Chatterjee
Filmmaker & Author

Contents

Foreword

India is a land of stories—ancient, profound, and mystical. From the majestic Himalayas to the sacred rivers, every corner of this vast country is steeped in legends that have been passed down through generations. These stories are not just tales; they are the soul of our culture, the essence of our beliefs, and the mirror of our identity.

In writing *Yakshini*, I have attempted to delve into one such legend that has been whispered across time, a tale that intertwines the mystical with the real, the past with the present. This book is not just a story but an exploration of the deep-rooted cultural heritage that defines India.

As a filmmaker and editor, I have always been fascinated by the power of narrative—how a story can transport us to another world, evoke deep emotions, and make us reflect on our own lives. With *Yakshini*, I wanted to take this fascination a step further by weaving a tale that captures the essence of India's spiritual and mythological richness.

Before *Yakshini*, I had the pleasure of writing *Samaykaal*, a novel that explored the concept of time travel while paying tribute to the eternal values of Sanatan Dharma. *Samaykaal* was a journey through time, blending science fiction with the timeless teachings of our ancestors. It was an ode to the wisdom of our past and a reminder of the eternal truths that guide us.

Yakshini, on the other hand, is an exploration of the supernatural, rooted in the legends that have shaped our understanding of the world. It is a story of power, mystery, and the unbreakable bond between the seen and the unseen. Through this book, I hope to bring to light the fascinating cultural legends of India that the world deserves to know.

India is not just a country; it is a treasure trove of stories waiting to be discovered. With *Yakshini*, I invite you to embark on a journey into the heart of these legends, to experience the magic, the mystery, and the timeless wisdom that has made India the land of stories.

I hope this book inspires you to look beyond the ordinary, to explore the extraordinary, and to discover the profound beauty of our cultural heritage.

Thank you for joining me on this journey.

Rahul Chatterjee

Filmmaker & Author

Preface

The idea of writing *Yakshini* came to me during one of those quiet moments when the mind wanders freely, unburdened by the demands of everyday life. As a filmmaker and editor, I have always been drawn to stories—particularly those that delve into the depths of human experience, those that explore the unseen and the mysterious. India, with its vast and diverse cultural heritage, is a land where such stories abound.

In the course of my work, I've often found myself reflecting on the tales that shaped my childhood, the myths and legends that were woven into the fabric of my upbringing. These stories, told and retold over centuries, are more than mere folklore. They are the lifeblood of our culture, connecting us to our roots, our ancestors, and our identity. And yet, many of these stories remain hidden, known only to a few or passed down in hushed whispers. The world knows India for its history, its diversity, and its spirituality, but there is so much more to discover—so much more that deserves to be shared.

Yakshini is my attempt to bring one such legend to light, to share with the world a story that is as haunting as it is beautiful, as mysterious as it is enlightening. It is a tale that merges the ancient with the contemporary, the real with the mystical. At its core, *Yakshini* is a story about power—power that transcends time and space, that bridges the gap between the material and the spiritual.

Before writing *Yakshini*, I explored another intriguing concept in my novel *Samaykaal*. That book was an ode to time travel, a tribute to the timeless wisdom of our Sanatan Dharma. In *Samaykaal*, I sought to capture the essence of India's spiritual teachings through the lens of science fiction, blending the old with the new in a way that honors our past while imagining our future.

With *Yakshini*, I wanted to take a different approach—to dive into the supernatural, to explore the myths that lurk in the shadows of our collective consciousness. This book is not just a story; it's an exploration of the unknown, an invitation to question the boundaries of reality as we know it.

Writing *Yakshini* has been an exhilarating journey, one that has deepened my appreciation for the rich tapestry of Indian culture. It is my hope that this book will resonate with you, that it will spark your curiosity, and that it will invite you to look at the world around you with fresh eyes.

India is a land of infinite stories, and *Yakshini* is but one of them. I am grateful to be able to share it with you, and I hope that it inspires you to seek out the countless other tales that await discovery.

Thank you for allowing me to take you on this journey.

Rahul Chatterjee

Filmmaker & Author

Acknowledgements

Writing *Yakshini* has been an incredible journey, and it would not have been possible without the support and encouragement of many people who walked alongside me on this path.

First and foremost, I want to express my deepest gratitude to my family for their unwavering support and love. To my parents, who have always encouraged me to pursue my passion for storytelling, and to my sister, Pankhuri Awasthy Rode, whose wisdom and creativity continue to inspire me every day—thank you for being my pillars of strength.

A heartfelt thanks to my friends and colleagues in the film industry, who have provided invaluable feedback and motivation throughout the writing process. Your insights have enriched this story in ways that I could not have imagined.

I am immensely grateful to my editors and publishing team, whose dedication and hard work have brought *Yakshini* to life. Your meticulous attention to detail and belief in this project have been instrumental in shaping the final product.

To my readers, who have embraced my previous work, *Samaykaal*, with such enthusiasm—thank you for your continued support. Your encouragement has fueled my desire to delve deeper into the rich cultural stories of our land and share them with the world.

Lastly, I would like to extend my gratitude to the countless storytellers, myth-makers, and historians who have preserved the legends and folklore of India. It is your work that has inspired me to write *Yakshini* and to celebrate the timeless narratives that define our heritage.

Thank you all for being a part of this journey. I am truly humbled by the love and support I have received, and I look forward to sharing more stories with you in the future.

With heartfelt appreciation,

Rahul Chatterjee

Filmmaker & Author

Prologue

The winds howled through the dense forest, carrying with them whispers of forgotten times. The night was dark, with only the faintest sliver of the moon piercing through the thick canopy of trees. In the stillness of the ancient woods, time itself seemed to stand still, as if the forest were holding its breath, waiting for something—something that had been buried in the depths of history to resurface.

Centuries ago, this land was a place of peace and prosperity, a small but thriving kingdom known as Sayal. It was a place where the earth was fertile, the rivers were bountiful, and the people lived in harmony with nature. But Sayal was more than just a prosperous kingdom; it was a place of mystery, guarded by forces that no man could comprehend. The elders spoke of a power that resided deep within the land—a power so ancient and so potent that it could alter the very fabric of reality.

In 1724, the tranquility of Sayal was shattered by the ambitions of a ruthless Afghan marauder. His name was whispered in fear across the lands, for his armies were vast and his cruelty unmatched. This invader, driven by greed and a thirst for power, sought to claim not just the riches of India but the mystical force that was said to reside in Sayal. He believed that with this power, he could bend even death to his will, making himself invincible, a ruler of both men and gods.

With an army of half a million strong, he sent his most trusted general to conquer the small kingdom. But the moment his soldiers set foot on Sayal's soil, they were met with something they had not anticipated—something far beyond the realm of human understanding. The great army, unstoppable in its might, vanished without a trace, leaving behind only the echoes of their screams carried on the wind.

The invader's dreams of becoming the Sultan of India crumbled into dust, as did his sanity. He returned to his homeland, a broken man, haunted by the horrors he had unleashed but could not control. The power he had sought remained out of reach, hidden within the depths of Sayal, guarded by forces that were as ancient as the earth itself.

The tale of Sayal and its mysterious protector faded into legend, a story told around firesides, a warning of the dangers of ambition and greed. But the land remembered. The power remained, waiting, watching, as the world around it changed, as kingdoms rose and fell, as centuries passed.

And now, in the present day, the whispers have begun anew. There are those who seek the power of Sayal once more, driven by the same desires that led the Afghan invader to his doom. But the land is not defenseless. It has its guardians—those who have been chosen to protect the secrets of the past, to ensure that the power remains hidden from those who would misuse it.

In the shadows of the forest, something stirs. The time has come for the legend to awaken, for the secrets of Sayal to be revealed. But those who seek the power must be wary, for the price of ambition is high, and the forces that guard the ancient land are unforgiving.

The stage is set, and the players are in motion. The story of *Yakshini* is about to begin.

Message To The Audience:

Dear Readers,

We would like to clarify that the mythology and history presented in the story Yakshini are entirely fictional and created for the purpose of this novel. This tale does not reflect or represent the actual history of India or the glorious traditions of Sanatan Dharma. The characters, events, and settings have been crafted purely for entertainment and are not based on real historical or religious accounts.

Our intention is to weave an engaging narrative of imagination, blending elements of fantasy and fiction. We deeply respect and honor India's rich cultural heritage and Sanatan Dharma, and we encourage readers to approach this story with an open mind, understanding that it is a work of fiction meant to inspire creativity and enjoyment.

Thank you for your understanding and support.

Warm regards,

The Yakshini Team

ONE

"THE NIGHTMARE"

The scorching heat of May 2021 baked the streets of Delhi. The world was still reeling from the devastation of the COVID-19 pandemic. A Sky Air Airlines flight from London was nearing its descent at Indira Gandhi International Airport. In a small, dimly lit flat in Old Delhi, Usman Qureshi's hacker den was alive with buzzing computers and flashing monitors. The place felt like the center of a storm, and at its eye was Usman, fast asleep on his bed—until a series of alerts snapped him awake. His phone, laptop, and desktop screens flared up, all displaying the same message: a marked passport had been scanned.Usman's heart raced as he recognized the name. The owner of the passport was about to land in Delhi. Without wasting a second, he grabbed his phone and dialed a number. His fingers trembled as the call connected.

Usman (excited, almost breathless):
"Boss... Boss, you won't believe what I've just found!"

Cut to:

A dimly lit, high-security office. ACHARYA, the most feared figure in India, sat at the head of a table. Surrounding him were the most notorious criminals from around the country and beyond. But despite the heavy atmosphere, Acharya's focus was on the phone call with his hacker.

Acharya (cold and deliberate):

"Usman, speak wisely. You know the consequences of wasting my time."

Usman (urgently):

"Sir, this is huge. The special guest you've been waiting for all these years... Robert Richardson's granddaughter... she's returning to India. She's landing in Delhi as we speak."Acharya's face darkened, a sinister smile playing on his lips.Acharya (to the room):

"Gentlemen, it seems the time has come. The guest we've been waiting for is finally here. The game is about to begin."

Back to:

Usman frantically worked on his computer, pulling up deeper information. His fingers flew over the keyboard as encrypted messages began appearing on his screen. Something about the Richardson family—this wasn't just a visit. There was a dark conspiracy at play.Usman (into the phone):

"Boss... it's not just a reunion. I'm seeing encrypted messages. This is a setup—something bigger is happening." Acharya (calmly, yet dangerously):

"Usman, get me everything you've got. We'll make sure her return is... unforgettable."As Usman continued to dig, his computer started to glitch. Lines of code flickered and then—blackout. His entire system shut down.

Silence.

But this was no ordinary glitch. This was a warning.Unbeknownst to Usman, what had begun 300 years ago with a curse was now coming full circle. The Richardson family's return wasn't just tied to the modern-day, but to an ancient curse—one that was destined to unravel, starting with this very moment.

The storm had begun.

The story of Princess Durgawati has been passed down through generations, shrouded in mystery and legend. Her name alone evokes awe and wonder, for she was no ordinary princess—she was said to be the incarnation of the goddess Durga herself, born under the blessings of the gods. The people of her kingdom often spoke of how her parents, after years of prayer and devotion, were granted a divine boon, leading to her miraculous birth. Her arrival was seen as a sign that she was destined to protect her people and lead them to greatness.

From a young age, Durgawati displayed extraordinary qualities. Her beauty was as radiant as the morning sun, her grace unmatched, and her intelligence beyond her years. But it was her strength that truly set her apart. She was trained in the arts of warfare alongside the greatest warriors of her time. Archery, swordsmanship, and combat strategies came to her as naturally as breathing. It was said that when she rode into battle, she did so with the fierceness and precision of the goddess Durga herself, earning her the title "Warrior Princess."

Despite her youth, Durgawati became a legend in her own time. Tales of her victories in battle spread far and wide. She defended her kingdom from invaders with unparalleled courage, leading her armies into battle without hesitation. Kingdoms that once sought to conquer her land soon learned to fear her name. In the halls of her palace, even the greatest warriors bowed before her, acknowledging her as not just their ruler, but their protector and guide.

But as powerful and beloved as she was, there was a side to Durgawati that remained a mystery to all. She was a solitary figure, rarely seen outside of the battlefield or court. While her people adored her, they whispered of a sadness in her eyes, a weight she carried that no one could understand. Some said she had been cursed by a jealous sorcerer, others believed she had visions of a great disaster to come. But no one dared to question her, for Durgawati was not just their ruler—she was the embodiment of their faith and hope.

Then, one day, something happened that no one could have predicted. Princess Durgawati disappeared.

It was sudden, without warning. One evening she was in her palace, discussing matters of state with her ministers. By the next morning, she was gone. There were no signs of struggle, no trace of where she might have gone. Her closest attendants were baffled. Her generals were in shock. How could the strongest, most powerful woman in the land vanish without a single clue?

The kingdom was thrown into chaos. Search parties were sent to every corner of the realm. Scouts combed the forests, mountains, and rivers, but they found nothing. Her chambers were searched for any hidden messages, but there were none. The people, in their desperation, turned to oracles and sages, hoping that divine intervention might reveal her fate. But even the gods were silent.

Rumors quickly began to spread. Some claimed that Durgawati had been taken by the gods, as a reward for her unmatched valor and virtue. Others believed that she had fled, tired of the burden of leadership and the weight of her responsibilities. A darker theory suggested that enemies, long hiding in the shadows, had finally found a way to capture her. But no matter the theory, one fact remained: the beloved princess had vanished, and with her, the light of the kingdom dimmed.

Years passed, and the mystery deepened. Stories of her began to turn into legends, each one more fantastical than the last. Some said that she had taken on a new form, roaming the world in disguise, watching over her people from afar. Others believed she was trapped in another realm, waiting for the day she would return to reclaim her throne. Still, others whispered of an ancient curse, one that had been placed on her bloodline, finally coming to pass.

But despite all the tales and speculation, no one truly knew what happened to Durgawati. The secret of her disappearance has remained one of the greatest unsolved mysteries for generations. Even today, scholars, adventurers, and historians search for clues, hoping to be the ones to unlock the truth behind her sudden vanishing.

Was she a mortal princess, destined to live a brief but extraordinary life? Or was she something more—an immortal force, bound by powers beyond human comprehension, waiting for the moment she will return to her kingdom and her people?

The answers are buried in the sands of time, hidden from the world. And so, the legend of Princess Durgawati lives on, a tale of beauty, power, and an unsolved mystery that continues to haunt the imaginations of all who hear her story.

The Doom of Sayal Kingdom

It was a crisp autumn morning in the 18th century, and the Sayal Kingdom hummed with the usual sounds of life. Farmers tilled their fields, oxen ploughed the earth, and the village bustled with quiet productivity. The golden sun bathed the land in warmth, but as the hours passed, something felt off.

The farmers were the first to notice it—an unnatural stillness in the air. Birds stopped singing, and the winds that usually swept the plains came to a sudden halt. Then, out of nowhere, the sky began to darken. It wasn't like the coming of a storm; it was as if the heavens themselves had turned black. The villagers and farmers looked up in confusion, shielding their eyes as a thick blanket of dark clouds gathered, circling ominously above the hilltop where the grand palace of the Sayal King sat, overlooking the kingdom like a sentinel.

The ground trembled.

Up on the hill, the palace, once a symbol of strength and glory, began to shake. Servants and soldiers inside the royal grounds felt the tremors before they heard them. Dishes clattered, and chandeliers swung violently as the foundation of the ancient structure groaned under some unseen pressure. Panic erupted. Footsteps echoed in the corridors as the soldiers abandoned their posts, rushing about in confusion. Servants screamed, their voices swallowed by the roar of the earth beneath them.

From the fields below, the farmers watched helplessly as a vortex of clouds swirled faster and faster above the palace. All at once, a blinding flash of light tore through the heavens. A bolt of lightning, as thick as a tree trunk, crashed down upon the mountain peak where the Sayal palace stood. The impact was deafening, and it split the air with such force that the ground shook for miles around.

Inside the palace, chaos turned to terror as the walls shook, and the great pillars of the throne room cracked. Soldiers and servants ran frantically, but amidst the pandemonium, the King of Sayal remained seated on his throne. His expression, strangely calm, suggested that he knew. He had foreseen this moment—this divine wrath.

Lightning struck again, and this time it hit the palace directly, engulfing its tall spires in flames. Smoke billowed into the blackened sky as the fire spread rapidly through the royal chambers. From the fields below, the farmers watched in horror as the once-mighty palace began to crumble, flames licking its walls like a vengeful beast.

"The gods," someone whispered in fear. "The gods are angry with us."

As the palace burned, the King did not move. He sat, motionless, as the roof above him began to cave, the fire inching closer. There was no fear in his eyes, only a cold acceptance. He knew.

But why?

The Ominous Prophecy

The King's knowledge of what was happening was no accident. Weeks before this disaster, strange omens had begun to manifest in the Sayal Kingdom. Animals started acting erratically, with horses refusing to leave their stables and dogs howling endlessly at the sky. Crops that once thrived turned barren overnight, and the rivers that fed the kingdom ran slower and darker, as if tainted by some unseen curse. The court astrologers, who were normally called to offer guidance in times of uncertainty, grew uneasy as their charts revealed a looming disaster—one they could not fully explain.

"Your Majesty," the chief astrologer, Varuna, had said during a private audience, his voice trembling. "The stars are... misaligned. I've never seen anything like it. Mars and Saturn are converging in the House of Death. This is a bad omen—an omen of destruction."

The King had listened in silence. His face, usually so composed, betrayed nothing of the unease that rippled through his court. But in his heart, he knew Varuna's warnings were not just empty superstition. The King had his own source of knowledge, one far older and more mysterious than any astrologer could comprehend.

In the deepest chamber of the palace, hidden away from the eyes of the court and even the royal family, lay an ancient relic—a stone tablet, etched with symbols from a forgotten time. Passed down from king to king, this tablet was said to contain the fate of the Sayal Dynasty, recorded by an ancient seer who had foreseen both the rise and fall of their line.

The King had consulted this tablet many times over the years, but recently, something had changed. The once stable and clear inscriptions had begun to shift. At first, it was subtle—a symbol out of place, a line that seemed longer than before. But as the days passed, the changes became more pronounced. Entire sections of the prophecy were rewritten before the King's eyes, and a single word appeared more frequently than any other: "End."

It was then that he understood. The fate of his kingdom was sealed, and no amount of preparation or prayer could change what was to come.

The Forgotten Curse

Centuries before the Sayal Kingdom had been founded, the land it now occupied had been home to another civilization, one long forgotten by the world. Legend had it that this civilization, known as the Aghrians, had angered the gods through their arrogance. They had built a magnificent city on the very same hill where the Sayal palace now stood, and they believed themselves invincible—above both man and god.

But their pride led to their downfall. A great calamity befell the Aghrians, wiping their city from existence. Some said it was an earthquake, others believed it was a plague sent by the gods. Whatever it was, the entire civilization was wiped out in a single night. All that remained were the ruins, buried deep beneath the earth, and the whispered curse that anyone who dared to rebuild on that land would suffer the same fate.

The founders of the Sayal Dynasty, however, had dismissed the warnings. They believed themselves more powerful, more favored by the gods than the Aghrians had been. So, they built their palace atop the cursed hill, unaware—or perhaps in denial—of the forces that still lingered below.

For centuries, the curse remained dormant. The Sayal kings ruled in peace, their kingdom flourishing. But like all curses, it was only a matter of time before it resurfaced.

And now, as the palace burned, it was clear that the curse had awoken with a vengeance.

The People's Despair

As the sky continued to darken, the people of Sayal looked on in horror from the villages below. Mothers clutched their children, while men stood helplessly, unsure of what to do. They had never seen anything like this. Some dropped to their knees, praying to the gods for mercy, while others ran in panic, convinced that the end of the world had come.

Among the farmers, there was an old man named Ramu, a man who had lived through many seasons and seen his share of both prosperity and hardship in the kingdom. But this... this was unlike anything he had ever witnessed.

He turned to the others, his voice shaking with fear and wisdom. "This is no ordinary storm," he said. "The gods are punishing us. The King has brought this upon us."

"But why, Ramu?" a young farmer asked, his face pale with fear. "What have we done?"

"It is not what we have done," Ramu replied. "It is what the King has hidden from us. There is a darkness in that palace, a secret that was never meant to be uncovered."

Before he could explain further, another flash of lightning lit up the sky, followed by an earth-shattering boom. The ground beneath them shook violently, causing the villagers to fall to their knees. The fire on the hilltop grew brighter, and from the distance, the cries of those trapped in the palace could be heard.

"Run!" someone shouted. "We must flee the kingdom!"

But there was nowhere to run. The black clouds had now stretched across the entire horizon, trapping the kingdom in a suffocating blanket of darkness. The once-clear rivers that flowed through the land began to churn violently, their waters turning a sickly shade of red.

The people of Sayal were trapped. There would be no escape from what was coming.

The King's Final Act

Back in the throne room, the King remained unmoved as the fire consumed the palace around him. His soldiers had long since abandoned their posts, and the servants had fled. Only the King remained, watching as the flames crept closer.

He reached into the folds of his robe and pulled out a small, ornate key. It was the key to the hidden chamber where the ancient tablet lay. With slow, deliberate movements, the King rose from his throne and began walking through the crumbling corridors of the palace, the heat of the fire growing more intense with each step.

As he approached the door to the hidden chamber, the floor beneath him trembled violently, threatening to collapse at any moment. But the King was determined. He unlocked the door and stepped inside, his eyes falling on the ancient tablet that had haunted him for so many years.

The symbols on the tablet were now glowing, pulsing with a strange, otherworldly light. The word "End" was etched across the entire surface, and as the King approached, the light grew brighter, almost blinding.

With a trembling hand, the King reached out and touched the tablet.

At that moment, the ground beneath the palace gave way entirely. The mountain itself seemed to split open, swallowing the once-grand structure whole. From the village below, the people watched in horror as the palace, the King, and everything within it disappeared into the earth, consumed by the curse that had been waiting for centuries to claim its due.

Aftermath: A Kingdom Lost

When the dust finally settled, the Sayal Kingdom was no more. The palace had been reduced to rubble, and the land around it lay barren and lifeless. The once-thriving villages were now eerily quiet, their inhabitants too afraid to speak of what had happened.

Days turned into weeks, and the black clouds that had once hung over the kingdom slowly began to dissipate. But the damage had been done. The rivers remained poisoned, the crops refused to grow, and the animals that had once roamed the land had disappeared.

Some of the villagers tried to rebuild, but it was futile. The land had been cursed, just as the Aghrians had been, and there was no reversing the destruction that had been wrought.

As the years passed, the story of the Sayal Kingdom became nothing more than a cautionary tale, a warning to those who dared to defy the gods. The ruins of the palace became a forbidden place, shrouded in mystery and fear.

And so, the Kingdom of Sayal was lost to history, its fate sealed by the arrogance of its rulers and the wrath of the gods.

But deep beneath the earth, where the remains of the palace lay buried, the ancient curse still lingered, waiting for the next fool who would dare to challenge it.

The Awakening of the Curse

For generations, the Sayal Kingdom was remembered only in whispers, its tragic end serving as a grim reminder of the wrath that had once been unleashed upon the land. Few dared to speak of the ancient curse that had consumed the kingdom, and even fewer dared to venture near the ruins of the palace, which had long since been swallowed by the earth.

But the curse had not been forgotten entirely.

In a distant village, far from the borders of what had once been Sayal, a group of scholars had become obsessed with the legends surrounding the fallen kingdom. Among them was a young historian named Aarya, whose fascination with the curse had consumed her for years.

Aarya had spent her entire life studying ancient texts and forgotten myths, and she was convinced that the key to understanding the downfall of Sayal lay hidden in the ruins of the palace. Despite the warnings of her fellow scholars, Aarya set out on a perilous journey to the site of the cursed kingdom, determined to uncover the truth.

As she approached the desolate landscape that had once been Sayal, Aarya felt a chill in the air. The land was barren, the trees long dead, and the rivers had turned to dry, cracked beds. The ground beneath her feet was hard and unforgiving, and the sky above was a dull, lifeless gray.

But Aarya pressed on, her determination unshaken. She had come too far to turn back now.

When she finally reached the site of the palace, she found nothing but rubble and debris. The once-magnificent structure had been reduced to a pile of stones, half-buried beneath the earth. But Aarya was undeterred. She knew that the secrets of the curse lay deeper beneath the surface, waiting to be uncovered.

With great effort, Aarya began to dig through the rubble, her hands raw and bloody from the sharp stones. Hours turned into days, and still, she found nothing. But just as she was about to give up, her hand brushed against something cold and hard.

It was the ancient tablet.

The symbols on its surface had long since faded, but Aarya could feel the power that still radiated from the stone. As she lifted the tablet from the earth, she felt a strange energy course through her body, and the ground beneath her began to tremble.

The curse had been awakened.

In the time when Heaven gleamed with the unblemished purity of the gods, and the mortal realm was but a faint whisper of creation, Yakshini shone brighter than any celestial being. As an attendant of Goddess Maha Shakti, the almighty force of the cosmos, Yakshini was revered for her beauty, intelligence, and dedication. Her heart had been pure once, and she was entrusted with guarding Heaven's most precious treasures, vast chambers filled with gold, gemstones, and artifacts too powerful for mortal eyes to behold.

But where divinity and duty were expected to prevail, a subtle greed began to take root in her soul. Yakshini's gaze lingered too long on the treasures she guarded. The gold gleamed under her watchful eye, calling to her in ways she didn't understand at first. Admiration soon twisted into desire, and desire quickly became an insatiable hunger.

She could no longer resist the pull of the gold, whispering promises of power and fulfillment. One day, as the celestial halls were silent and no eyes fell upon her, Yakshini succumbed to the temptation. Her hand hovered over a piece of gold, trembling, as though touching it would change her forever. And when her fingers finally grasped the cold, gleaming metal, a rush of power coursed through her veins.

She thought she could stop after taking just a few pieces, hiding them in the shadows of her chambers. But with each passing day, the hunger grew more intense. Her divine light, once radiant, began to dim, and her beauty was tainted by the greed that consumed her heart.

Yakshini's fall did not go unnoticed for long. The gods whispered of her growing distance, her neglect of duty, and her fading radiance. But it was Maha Shakti herself, the all-knowing, who finally saw the truth in Yakshini's heart.

One fateful day, Yakshini was summoned to the celestial court. The skies above Heaven dimmed as a storm of divine judgment loomed on the horizon. In the grand halls of the gods, Maha Shakti sat upon her throne, her eyes burning with the fire of justice.

"Yakshini," Maha Shakti's voice thundered, echoing through the chambers, "you were entrusted with the wealth of Heaven, with treasures beyond mortal comprehension. But you have let your greed consume you. You have betrayed the divine trust placed in you, and for that, there will be no mercy."

Yakshini, trembling in fear, fell to her knees before the almighty goddess. "Forgive me, great Maha Shakti," she pleaded, her voice barely above a whisper. "I was blinded by desire, but I can return what I have taken. Please, grant me redemption."

But Maha Shakti's gaze remained cold and unyielding. "The gold you stole has cursed you, Yakshini. It has twisted your soul beyond recognition. Redemption is not for those who seek it only in the face of punishment."

With a wave of her hand, Maha Shakti unleashed the storm. Divine energy surged through the heavens, and Yakshini screamed as chains of light bound her, their searing heat a constant reminder of her sin. Her once-beautiful form was twisted by the curse of greed, her face marred and her wings withered.

"For your betrayal, you shall be cast out of Heaven," Maha Shakti declared. "You will be imprisoned in the mortal realm, bound by the very gold you coveted. You will be cursed to wait for centuries, yearning for freedom. And when that day comes, the skies will turn red, and acid rain will pour from the heavens. It will be a sign that the world trembles before your hunger once more."

With those final words, Maha Shakti banished Yakshini from the celestial realm. The goddess fell from Heaven, her screams of agony echoing through the stars as she plummeted to the earth below.

Yakshini's fall ended in the depths of the earth, in a desolate wasteland where nothing grew and no life flourished. There, the ground split open, and she was swallowed by the earth, imprisoned in a cavern lined with the very gold she had once coveted. The cursed gold formed chains around her, binding her to the cavern's walls, trapping her in a prison from which there was no escape.

The divine chains of greed wrapped around her soul, tightening with every movement, every thought of freedom. The once-beautiful goddess was now a twisted shadow, her body contorted by the weight of her sin. The gold, once a symbol of power, was now her tormentor, gleaming mockingly in the darkness of her prison.

As the centuries passed, the world above moved on. Mortals built empires, civilizations rose and fell, but Yakshini remained forgotten, trapped beneath the earth. Her hunger for gold, for freedom, never ceased. It festered in the dark, growing stronger with each passing year.

But there was something more than greed now—there was rage. Rage at the gods who had forsaken her, at Maha Shakti for casting her down, at the mortals who lived blissfully unaware of her suffering. She longed not just for freedom, but for vengeance.

And yet, even in her fury, a part of her waited. She knew the prophecy well—the day when the skies would turn red, and the rain would burn the earth. That day would mark her release from this prison. And when it came, she would rise again.

In the modern era, long after Yakshini's fall from grace, the earth above her prison remained barren. But deep underground, beneath layers of stone and rock, something stirred.

One day, a group of miners, unaware of the ancient curse they were about to awaken, stumbled upon a strange, shimmering gold deposit. The gold was unlike anything they had ever seen, glowing with an unnatural light. Greed filled their hearts as they clawed at the walls, desperate to claim the treasure for themselves.

The moment their tools struck the cursed gold, a dark force began to seep from the earth. The ground trembled, and the skies above began to shift. Clouds swirled in unnatural patterns, and the sun dimmed, casting the world in an eerie red light.

The prophecy had begun.

Deep within her prison, Yakshini stirred. Her eyes, long closed in her cursed slumber, snapped open. She felt the chains that bound her beginning to weaken, the curse loosening its grip. For the first time in centuries, she felt hope—hope that her freedom was near.

But as the prophecy foretold, her release would not come without consequence. The skies above turned blood-red, and a fierce storm gathered on the horizon. The first drops of acid rain fell, burning the earth where they landed. The world above trembled in fear, unaware of the ancient evil stirring beneath their feet.

Yakshini's heart raced as she felt the power of the prophecy drawing closer. Her prison walls trembled, the gold chains weakening with each passing moment. She could feel the hunger within her rising, the same hunger that had led to her downfall.

But even as she waited for the final moment of her release, she knew that her fate was not entirely in her hands. The prophecy was clear—when she was freed, she would have to choose. She could either seek redemption, finally letting go of her greed and accepting her punishment, or she could give in to the hunger once more, unleashing a fury upon the world that would rival the gods themselves.

For now, she remained trapped, her body bound by the cursed gold, her mind teetering between madness and clarity. The world above began to crumble, and mortals whispered of the strange red skies and the burning rain.

But Yakshini knew the truth. This was only the beginning. The final chains were breaking, and soon, she would be free.

And so, Yakshini waited.

The storm above grew fiercer, and the acid rain poured down in torrents, scorching the earth and turning rivers into rivers of poison. The mortals below screamed in terror, but Yakshini could not hear them. She was deep beneath the earth, trapped in the darkness, listening only to the beat of her own heart and the steady drip of the cursed rain above her.

Her fingers twitched as she felt the final strands of her prison beginning to unravel. She could sense the world trembling in anticipation of her release. But still, she waited.

In her mind, she replayed the words of Maha Shakti over and over again. "When the sky turns red, and the rain burns the earth, you will be free."

The prophecy was coming true, just as it had been foretold. But what would happen when she finally broke free? Would she find redemption, or would she succumb to the greed that still gnawed at her soul?

The answer remained elusive, even to her.

And so, Yakshini waited in the darkness, her heart filled with equal parts hunger and hope, trapped between two fates. The moment of her freedom was near, but the choice of what to do with it would be hers alone.

And the world above would soon find out which path she chose.

To be continued...

Part 1: The Quiet Town of Sayal

In the quaint, historical town of Sayal, Assam, life moved at a gentle pace. Nestled amidst lush green fields and towering mountains, the town was a canvas of serene beauty. The sun-drenched days were spent in the bustling markets, where vendors sold everything from vibrant textiles to fragrant spices. In the evenings, families gathered on porches, exchanging stories under the watchful eyes of ancient trees that had stood for centuries. But as night fell, the serenity of Sayal transformed into an unsettling stillness, for the townsfolk whispered of a haunted past that lingered in the shadows.

Renu, a dedicated researcher, had moved to Sayal a year ago to work at the local university's botanical lab. She was drawn to the area's diverse flora and ancient remedies, hoping to uncover the secrets hidden within the forest. An ambitious woman in her early thirties, Renu often spent late nights in the lab, captivated by her research. Despite her dedication, the town's quietude sometimes gnawed at her, filling her with a sense of isolation.

Her husband, Vikram, a writer, often worried about her late nights. He believed that the stillness of Sayal had a weight to it, something that pressed down on those who lingered in it too long. "It's not safe to drive alone at night," he would often say, concern etched on his face. Renu would laugh it off, assuring him that she was careful and alert.

But as the weeks passed, the weight of the town's silence became palpable to Renu. It was as if the very air around her thickened with unspoken stories—tales of loss, betrayal, and the supernatural.

Part 2: The Night of Shadows

On one bleak Friday night, as the clock struck 11, Renu found herself finishing up in the lab. The fluorescent lights flickered overhead, casting a ghostly glow on the papers scattered across her desk. The aroma of formaldehyde lingered in the air, but tonight it was overshadowed by an inexplicable sense of dread. She wrapped up her work and made a mental note to send the reports to her supervisor, Sharma sir, in the morning.

"Sorry, sweetheart," she said over the phone, attempting to soothe Vikram's annoyance. "I know you're angry with me, but I didn't realize how late it had gotten. Don't worry, I've prepared the report and will email it first thing."

"Renu, it's already late," Vikram replied, his voice a mixture of concern and frustration. "You should've left earlier."

"I will be home in about 15 minutes," she reassured him, trying to lighten the mood. "What? Where am I now?"

Renu glanced outside, her brow furrowing as she spotted the milestone marking the entrance to Judge Colony. **JJ Colony: 3 km.**

"That's strange," she thought, the gnawing sense of unease creeping back. "I must be tired."

With a firm resolve, she continued driving, determined to shake off the disorientation. But moments later, the same milestone appeared before her. **JJ Colony: 3 km.**

"No way!" she gasped, gripping the steering wheel tightly. "This is impossible."

Renu stopped her car on the deserted road, her heart racing. She leaned back, taking a moment to breathe, forcing herself to calm down. She knew she had taken the same route countless times before, but tonight felt different. The shadows cast by the trees seemed to stretch and distort, and the darkness felt heavier.

"Just a coincidence," she muttered, shaking her head. "I'll just drive home."

Determined, she pressed on, but the milestone repeated itself. Panic began to claw at her chest. "This can't be real," she thought, her breathing quickening. She stepped out of the car, desperate to clear her head.

The night air was cool, but the silence felt suffocating. As she stood there, she heard the rustle of leaves and a distant sound—an indistinguishable whispering that sent chills down her spine. She shook her head again, trying to dispel the feeling of dread.

Returning to her car, she resolved to call Vikram again, but as she reached for her phone, it slipped from her grasp, landing on the seat. Just then, the headlights illuminated a fleeting shadow darting behind the trees, and Renu's heart raced.

"Okay, I need to go home," she muttered, her resolve wavering.

*But as she climbed back into her car, the whispering returned, more pronounced now, echoing in her mind like a melody she couldn't quite grasp. She started the engine and sped off, adrenaline pumping through her veins, but the familiar sight of the **JJ Colony: 3 km** milestone appeared yet again.*

"I'm going crazy!" Renu yelled, slamming her hands on the steering wheel in frustration.

Part 3: The Woman in White

As she sat there, wrestling with her mounting panic, she decided to take a different route through a side road that veered into the forest. The branches of the trees stretched out like skeletal fingers, creating a canopy that blocked out the moonlight. The further she drove, the more isolated she felt, as if the town itself was fading away behind her.

The landscape around her shifted, becoming more sinister. Shadows flitted between the trees, and the whispering grew louder, more insistent. Renu could feel a presence, lurking just beyond her vision.

Suddenly, the car lights illuminated a figure standing by the side of the road—a woman clad in a white saree, her long hair cascading down her back. The woman's face was obscured, but Renu felt an inexplicable pull toward her.

Without thinking, Renu slowed her car and rolled down the window. "Excuse me, do you need help?" she called out, her voice trembling slightly.

The woman turned slowly, revealing hollow eyes that seemed to bore into Renu's soul. "Help?" the woman echoed, her voice barely a whisper. "You shouldn't be here. It's not safe."

"What do you mean?" Renu asked, her heart pounding. "Where is this? I need to get home."

The woman stepped closer, her movements fluid yet haunting. "Home? You don't belong here. Turn back before it's too late."

Suddenly, the whispers intensified, swirling around Renu like a tempest. Fear gripped her, and she slammed her foot on the accelerator, speeding away from the ghostly figure. She glanced back in the rearview mirror, but the woman had vanished, leaving nothing but darkness in her wake.

"Just a figment of my imagination," Renu told herself, desperate to quell the rising tide of panic.

But as she continued driving, she noticed something unsettling—the landscape around her had transformed. The familiar roads of Sayal were gone, replaced by a twisted version of the town, filled with dilapidated buildings and shadows that seemed to shift and pulse with malevolence.

Part 4: The Endless Loop

*Renu felt as though she were trapped in a nightmare, a cruel trick of fate that had locked her in an endless loop. She turned around, trying to retrace her steps, but each time she thought she was getting closer to home, the same **JJ Colony: 3 km** milestone appeared, mocking her attempts to escape.*

"Why can't I get out of here?" she yelled, tears streaming down her face. The sense of hopelessness washed over her, and despair clawed at her heart.

Desperate, she called Vikram again. "Please, I'm stuck!" she cried. "I can't get home. I don't know what's happening!"

"Renu, where are you?" he replied, his voice thick with worry. "Just stay in your car and lock the doors. I'll come find you."

Renu tried to calm herself, but the whispers echoed in her mind. She glanced around, feeling as if unseen eyes were watching her every move. Then, she saw a flicker of movement in the corner of her eye.

Turning her head, Renu saw the woman in white again, this time standing further down the road, gesturing for her to come closer.

"No! I won't go near you!" Renu shouted, locking the doors in terror. "Stay away from me!"

But the woman continued to beckon her, an ethereal smile gracing her lips. Renu felt a surge of anger and fear, and she stepped on the gas, the tires screeching as she raced away from the figure.

The world outside her window blurred into a kaleidoscope of darkness, and she realized that she was spiraling deeper into the nightmare. The once-familiar roads of Sayal had transformed into an alien landscape, and the haunting presence of the woman loomed large in her mind.

Part 5: The Reckoning

After what felt like hours of driving, Renu's resolve began to crumble. The weight of exhaustion pressed down on her, and her eyelids grew heavy. Just when she thought she might drift off, a loud crash startled her.

"Wake up, Renu!" she screamed at herself, shaking her head violently.

But it was too late. As she rubbed her eyes, she realized she had veered off the road, and her car had come to a halt in front of an old, dilapidated building. It appeared to be an abandoned house, its windows dark and empty like the hollow eyes of the woman.

"What is this place?" Renu wondered aloud, stepping out of the car against her better judgment.

The air was thick with silence, the only sound being the faint rustle of leaves. She walked closer to the building, drawn by an unseen force, her heart racing in her chest.

As she approached, she noticed something shimmering in the moonlight—a silver locket lying on the ground. Curious, Renu picked it up, its cool surface sending a shiver down her spine.

When she opened it, a photograph of a young woman stared back at her—the same woman from the road. Suddenly, the whispers grew louder, swirling around her like a hurricane. "You shouldn't be here," they chanted, their voices a cacophony of sorrow.

"Who are you?" Renu shouted, her voice breaking. "What do you want from me?"

In that moment, the shadows surrounding her coalesced into a figure—the woman in white. "You have to help me," she said, her voice resonating with urgency. "My name is Meera. I was lost here long ago, trapped between worlds. I need you to find my soul, buried beneath the weight of this town's history."

"What do you mean?" Renu stammered, her mind racing.

"The darkness here is alive. It feeds on fear and sorrow, trapping souls like mine. You have the power to free us, but you must confront the truth hidden in the depths of Sayal."

Part 6: The Journey Within

Renu's heart pounded in her chest as Meera's words echoed in her mind. "How can I help you?" she asked, her voice trembling.

"Listen to the whispers," Meera replied. "They will guide you to the truth. But be warned—the darkness will try to ensnare you. You must be strong."

Determined to uncover the mystery, Renu nodded. "I'll help you," she vowed, clutching the locket tightly in her hand.

With Meera as her guide, Renu stepped into the dilapidated house, where time seemed to stand still. Dust swirled in the air, and the floorboards creaked beneath her feet. The interior was a maze of forgotten memories, and every corner held secrets waiting to be uncovered.

As they ventured deeper into the house, Renu began to hear the whispers more clearly. They spoke of betrayal, loss, and unresolved pain, stories of the townsfolk who had suffered in silence.

"Listen carefully," Meera urged. "Each voice has a story to tell. You must find the source of the darkness that binds us."

The whispers grew louder, guiding Renu through darkened rooms filled with relics of the past. In one room, she discovered old photographs depicting the town's history—families celebrating festivals, couples in love, children playing. But as she examined them closely, she noticed a shadowy figure lurking in the background of each image, a dark silhouette that seemed to watch over the happiness with malevolence.

"Who is that?" Renu gasped, pointing to the figure in the photographs.

"That is the spirit of despair," Meera explained, her expression grave. "It feeds off the pain of the town, trapping souls within its grasp. You must confront it and break its hold on Sayal."

Part 7: The Confrontation

With newfound resolve, Renu pressed onward, following the whispers deeper into the house. They led her to a dark basement, where the air felt heavy with sorrow.

The shadows writhed around her, and Renu could sense the presence of the spirit lurking nearby. "I am here!" she called out, her voice steady despite the fear coursing through her. "Show yourself!"

In response, the air crackled with energy, and the shadow materialized before her—a dark, formless figure that seemed to pulsate with a hunger for despair.

"Foolish mortal," it hissed, its voice like a thousand whispers. "You dare to challenge me? I am the darkness that consumes this town. I will devour your hope, just as I have done to all who came before you."

"No!" Renu shouted, her voice ringing with defiance. "I won't let you take me or anyone else. I know your secrets, and I will expose you!"

With the locket clutched tightly in her hand, Renu felt a surge of strength. The photograph of Meera filled her mind, and she focused on the memories of joy, love, and resilience that the townsfolk had shared.

"I remember you!" she cried, the light of hope igniting within her. "You are not powerful—you are nothing without our fear!"

The shadow shrieked, its form flickering as Renu summoned the strength of the memories she had uncovered. "I release you!" she declared, her voice resonating with conviction.

Part 8: The Light

As Renu spoke those words, a brilliant light erupted from the locket, enveloping her in a warm embrace. The darkness writhed and twisted, its hold on the town weakening. The whispers transformed from fearful cries into songs of liberation, resonating through the very fabric of Sayal.

Renu felt the presence of the townsfolk around her, their spirits joining her in the fight against despair. "You are free!" she cried, the words echoing with power.

The shadow howled in rage, but Renu stood firm, embracing the light that surrounded her. With one final surge of energy, she released the locket, allowing its light to envelop the darkness *completely.*

As the shadows dissipated, Renu felt a sense of peace wash over her. The whispers faded into a soft melody, and the weight that had pressed upon her heart lifted.

"You did it," Meera said, her voice filled with gratitude. "You freed us."

"Thank you for guiding me," Renu replied, tears streaming down her face. "I couldn't have done it without you."

Part 9: The Return

*As the last remnants of darkness faded away, Renu found herself back in her car, parked on the familiar road leading to Sayal. The **JJ Colony: 3 km** milestone stood proudly before her, but this time it felt like a beacon of hope.*

Renu drove home, her heart lighter than it had been in weeks. She couldn't shake the feeling that something profound had shifted in Sayal, that the town was beginning to heal.

When she finally arrived home, Vikram was waiting for her, worry etched on his face. "Thank God you're safe!" he exclaimed, wrapping her in a tight embrace.

"I'm sorry for worrying you," Renu whispered, the warmth of his presence grounding her. "But I think I understand the town now."

As they settled down together, Renu recounted the events of the night—the woman in white, the whispers, the confrontation with the darkness. Vikram listened intently, his eyes wide with astonishment.

"You're a part of Sayal now," he said softly. "Its history, its struggles. You've become part of something greater."

Renu nodded, feeling a sense of belonging she had never known before. She had confronted her fears and emerged stronger, not only for herself but for the town that had once felt so alien.

Part 10: The Healing

In the days that followed, Renu felt a renewed purpose in her research. She began to work on a project focused on the history of Sayal, documenting the stories of its inhabitants and their resilience.

As she delved into the past, she uncovered the struggles and triumphs of the townsfolk—stories that had been buried under layers of pain and sorrow. With each narrative she unearthed, she felt the light of hope shining brighter within the town, as if the spirits of those lost were guiding her hand.

Vikram began writing a book inspired by Renu's journey, capturing the essence of Sayal's haunting beauty and the resilience of its people. They became a team, bound by their love and their shared mission to bring the town's stories to light.

Together, they organized community events, inviting residents to share their tales and honor the memories of those who had come before. Slowly but surely, the darkness that had loomed over Sayal began to lift, replaced by a sense of unity and hope.

Part 11: The Legacy

Months passed, and as the seasons changed, so too did Sayal. The town blossomed with life, its streets filled with laughter and love. Renu's work was celebrated, and Vikram's book garnered attention, bringing visitors who were eager to learn about the town's rich history.

And yet, Renu never forgot the woman in white, nor the darkness that had once threatened to consume Sayal. In her heart, she held a promise to honor the stories of those who had suffered, ensuring that the town's history would never be forgotten.

As she walked through the vibrant markets, surrounded by the sounds of joy and laughter, Renu felt a deep sense of peace. She had faced the shadows and emerged victorious, forever changed by the experience.

In the quiet moments, when the sun dipped below the horizon and the stars twinkled above, Renu would often visit the old house where the darkness had once thrived. There, she felt Meera's presence, a gentle reminder of the connection they shared.

The whispers had transformed into songs of hope, weaving through the very fabric of Sayal, creating a tapestry of resilience that would carry the town forward. Renu smiled, knowing that she had played a part in

that journey, a bridge between the past and the future.

And so, the legacy of Sayal continued to thrive, a testament to the power of love, hope, and the enduring strength of the human spirit. Renu had not only found herself in the heart of the town, but she had also become a beacon of light for all those who had been lost, guiding them toward the promise of a brighter tomorrow.

Part 12: Epilogue

Years later, Renu stood on the steps of her home, a beautiful garden blooming around her. Children played in the streets, their laughter filling the air, and the spirit of Sayal was alive with vibrancy.

She looked back at the journey that had brought her here—the fears she had conquered, the darkness she had faced, and the love that had blossomed in the heart of Sayal.

"Meera," she whispered, a soft smile gracing her lips. "Thank you for guiding me."

The air around her felt warm, as if the very essence of the town was embracing her, reminding her that she was never alone. She had become part of a legacy, one that would carry on for generations to come—a legacy of hope, love, and the enduring power of the human spirit to overcome even the darkest of nights.

And as the sun set, painting the sky in hues of orange and pink, Renu knew that the light of Sayal would forever shine bright, illuminating the path for all who dared to dream.

RAHUL CHATTERJEE

(While Renu's husband was talking to her on the phone, she suddenly felt someone's hot, heavy breath behind her, as if someone was standing right there, breathing down her neck. Terrified, she slowly turned around and saw the most horrifying sight of her life. A woman, dressed in red clothes soaked in blood, with dishevelled hair adorned with gleaming gold jewellery, was standing right behind her. The woman, with a terrifying expression, looked at Renu, extended her hand towards her, and in a chilling voice, said):

SCARY WOMAN (In a scary voice):

"Return to me... what is mine."

And then with fearful and trembling eyes the girl looked behind her towards her car in which a bag was kept, and then that terrible woman, walking fast, caught hold of the girl and gouged out her eyes with her hands and The girl's scream echoed throughout that Sangasan road.

'

TWO
YAKSHINI A LEGEND

In the early years of the 18th century, the Indian subcontinent was a vast tapestry of empires, petty kingdoms, and dynasties, each vying for supremacy over the others. The Mughal Empire, once the undisputed ruler of much of the region, had begun to decline, its authority fragmented by internal strife and the emergence of powerful regional leaders. Amid this backdrop of political instability and warfare, a man rose from the harsh, unforgiving mountains of Afghanistan—a man whose name would soon be feared across the entire subcontinent. His name was Azad Khan, and his reputation as a ruthless marauder would surpass even the most infamous conquerors in history.

Azad Khan was born in the rugged terrain of what is now southern Afghanistan, a land steeped in blood and conflict. From a young age, he had been shaped by the brutal realities of life in this inhospitable region. He came from a long line of warriors, men who had survived and thrived in the unforgiving environment by adhering to a code of strength and merciless ambition. However, Azad's hunger for power far exceeded that of his ancestors. He sought not just to rule over his tribal lands *but to carve out a kingdom that would span continents.*

In the mountains where he grew up, the shadows held secrets of a different kind, and the winds whispered tales of ancient gods and terrible curses. The stories of spirits that demanded respect and retribution were etched into the very fabric of his upbringing. It was these legends that shaped his understanding of power—not merely as dominion over land and people, but as something primal, dark, and formidable. As Azad's ambition festered, so did the echoes of these ancient stories, molding him into a man both feared and revered.

By his mid-twenties, Azad had already assembled a formidable army, recruiting fighters from various clans and ethnic groups across the region. These men were hardened warriors, skilled in the art of war and fiercely loyal to their leader. With his army in tow, Azad launched a series of audacious raids into the northern reaches of India, pillaging towns and cities, enslaving their inhabitants, and amassing vast wealth. His cruelty was legendary—no village, no fort, no temple was spared from his wrath. His very name became synonymous with terror; even the bravest men quaked at the thought of facing him.

Unlike other marauders of his time, Azad was not satisfied with the material spoils of conquest. He had heard rumors, whispered in the smoky halls of Kabul and Kandahar, of an ancient power hidden deep within the Indian subcontinent—a power that could transcend the temporal riches of gold and jewels. This power, it was said, would grant its possessor dominion over not only the earth but the very fabric of existence itself. It was not the riches of India that lured Azad to its gates; it was the promise of ultimate, otherworldly power.

Far from the centers of Mughal and Maratha power, nestled in the dense, mist-shrouded forests of northeastern India, lay the Sayal Kingdom. It was a small realm, unremarkable in terms of military might or political influence. Yet, what it lacked in earthly power, it more than made up for in its deep connection to the mystical forces that governed the world.

The history of Sayal stretched back millennia, long before the rise of the great Indian empires. According to ancient lore, the kingdom had been established by a lineage of priest-kings who had made a sacred pact with the divine. It was said that the kingdom's rulers were descendants of a demigod who had been granted dominion over the land by the gods themselves. In return, the people of Sayal were charged with guarding a secret of immense power—an artifact said to contain the essence of creation itself. This artifact, known only as "The Light of Amara," was said to be imbued with a radiant energy that could bend time, space, and the laws of nature to the will of its possessor.

Over the centuries, many had sought to discover the truth behind this legend. Scholars, mystics, and adventurers had traveled to Sayal, hoping to unlock its secrets. Few ever returned, and those who did spoke of strange occurrences—visions of divine beings, eerie sounds in the night, and a palpable sense of being watched. The land itself seemed to pulsate with an otherworldly energy, a force that defied understanding. The people of Sayal lived in harmony with this energy, worshipping the forgotten gods of the ancient world and performing rituals to maintain the balance between the material and spiritual realms. Their priests were the keepers of sacred knowledge, passed down through generations, and the land was dotted with temples and shrines dedicated to the old gods. The Sayalites believed that their kingdom was blessed, protected by a divine force that would defend them from any who sought to harm it.

Azad Khan had long heard the legends of the Sayal Kingdom. Tales of its mystical power had reached him from traders and spies who had ventured into the remote region. The idea of such a force—something beyond mere wealth or military power—ignited a burning desire within him. If he could possess this artifact, this "Light of Amara," he would not only rule over India but all of existence itself. His name would be remembered for eternity, not as a mere conqueror, but as a god-king who held the reins of the universe.

In the summer of 1724, Azad began to mobilize his forces. His army, now numbering over 500,000 soldiers, was the largest ever assembled in the region. It was a force composed of hardened Afghan warriors, tribal levies, and mercenaries from across Central Asia. These men were fiercely loyal to Azad, drawn to his charisma and his promise of boundless wealth and glory.

As preparations for the invasion began, Azad gathered his most trusted generals and advisors. Among them was his closest confidant, General Iqbal, a man known for his strategic brilliance and unshakable loyalty. Iqbal had served Azad for over a decade, leading many of his most successful campaigns. Together, they devised a plan to march on the Sayal Kingdom and seize its mystical power.

Azad's court was filled with excitement and anticipation. The promise of untold riches and power fueled the ambitions of his officers and soldiers. Yet, there were whispers among the more superstitious members of his court—whispers of the cursed land of Sayal, of ancient gods who would not take kindly to the desecration of their sacred realm. These murmurs were quickly silenced, however, by Azad's unwavering belief in his destiny. He was no mere man; he was a force of nature, destined to reshape the world in his image.

As the vast Afghan army began its march towards the Sayal Kingdom, the very earth seemed to tremble beneath the weight of their numbers. Villages were evacuated, and towns fortified as word of the approaching horde spread like wildfire. The rulers of neighboring kingdoms watched with bated breath, unsure of what to make of Azad's audacious campaign.

The march to Sayal took weeks, as the army crossed rivers, mountains, and forests. The landscape grew increasingly difficult as they approached the northeastern territories. The soldiers began to notice strange occurrences—unexplained whispers in the wind, shadows that seemed to move of their own accord, and a heavy sense of foreboding that hung over the land. As they neared the borders of Sayal, the weather began to change dramatically. Dark clouds gathered in the sky, and a bitter cold wind swept across the plains. It was as though nature itself was rebelling against the invaders, warning them of the dangers that lay ahead.

Despite these ominous signs, Azad remained resolute. He ordered his army to continue the march, determined to reach the heart of the Sayal Kingdom. As they crossed the border into Sayal, the soldiers were greeted by a sight that would haunt them for the rest of their lives. The once lush and vibrant landscape of Sayal had transformed into something otherworldly. The trees, once full of life, now appeared twisted and gnarled, their branches reaching out like skeletal hands. The air was thick with an oppressive energy, a force that seemed to press down on the soldiers, making it difficult to breathe.

The Afghan army continued to march, but their progress was slow. As night fell, strange phenomena began to occur. Soldiers reported seeing figures in the distance—shadowy beings that seemed to flicker in and out of existence. Others claimed to hear voices, whispering in a language they could not understand. Some even reported seeing visions of their own deaths, played out before their eyes like a twisted prophecy. The fear that had been simmering beneath the surface now began to boil over. Soldiers deserted in the dead of night, fleeing into the wilderness in the hopes of escaping whatever malevolent force had taken hold of the land. Those who remained were gripped by a growing sense of dread, their morale eroding with each passing day.

On the third day after crossing into Sayal, Azad and his army reached the outskirts of the kingdom's capital. The city, which had once been a beacon of civilization and culture, now lay in ruins. The streets were empty, and the buildings had crumbled into dust, as though some great force had wiped it from the face of the earth. It was here, at the heart of the Sayal Kingdom, that the true nature of the curse revealed itself.

As the Afghan army began to set up camp, a deafening silence fell over the land. It was as if time itself had paused, holding its breath in anticipation of what was to come. Azad Khan, resolute and driven by his insatiable hunger for power, ordered his soldiers to prepare for battle. He believed that the guardians of the Light of Amara would not yield easily, and he was determined to crush any opposition that dared to stand in his way.

As night descended upon the ruined city, the atmosphere grew heavier with tension. The soldiers, exhausted and on edge, gathered around campfires, sharing tales of their past victories. But the bravado soon faded as an unnatural fog rolled in, enveloping the camp in a thick shroud. The fog seemed to pulse with a life of its own, swirling and twisting as though it held hidden horrors within its depths.

Suddenly, a chilling scream shattered the silence. One of the soldiers, a seasoned warrior known for his bravery, had vanished without a trace. Panic rippled through the ranks as men rushed to find their missing comrade. They searched the fog-shrouded streets, calling out his name, but their voices were swallowed by the suffocating darkness. One by one, more soldiers began to disappear, taken by the very shadows that *surrounded them. Azad, witnessing the chaos unfold before him, felt a flicker of doubt creep into his heart. But he pushed it aside, convinced that he was destined to obtain the Light of Amara and reclaim control over his faltering army.*

As the night wore on, the remaining soldiers grew increasingly frantic, haunted by the specters that seemed to lurk just beyond the periphery of their vision. Whispers filled the air, indecipherable yet unsettling, and visions of ancient beings flickered in the mist, teasing the minds of the frightened warriors. It was clear that they were not alone in this cursed land; something was watching them, something ancient and malevolent.

On the dawn of the fourth day, as the sun struggled to break through the fog, Azad called a council of his remaining generals. He demanded to know what had happened to the men who had vanished and how they could counter this strange phenomenon. Yet, as his generals shared their fears, one voice rose above the rest—a young soldier who had once been a humble farmer before joining Azad's ranks. He spoke of the legends surrounding Sayal, warning of the wrath of the ancient guardians that protected the kingdom.

"The Sayalites have not abandoned their land," he said, trembling with fear. "They remain, watching us from the shadows, waiting for their moment to strike."

Azad, enraged by the soldier's cowardice, dismissed him as a fool, but doubt gnawed at him. He could feel the weight of the land pressing down on him, and for the first time, he began to question his decision to invade Sayal.

As the sun set on the fourth day, Azad ordered his remaining soldiers to gather their strength and prepare for an assault on what he believed to be the last stronghold of the Sayalite defenders. The people of Sayal, he reasoned, must be holed up in the ancient temple dedicated to the Light of Amara, the very artifact he had come to claim.

The temple was a magnificent structure, adorned with intricate carvings depicting the gods of the ancient world. It stood as a testament to the rich history of Sayal, but now it was a tomb, filled with secrets that had been lost to time.

As they approached the temple, an eerie silence enveloped the area. The air grew thick with a palpable energy, crackling like static electricity. Azad and his remaining generals stood at the temple's entrance, peering into the darkness that lay beyond. He could feel the weight of destiny upon his shoulders as he prepared to step into the unknown.

Yet, as they crossed the threshold into the temple, a blinding light erupted from within. It illuminated the entire chamber, revealing a vast hall filled with ancient relics and statues that seemed to come alive in the glow. At the center of the room, on a pedestal of stone, lay the Light of Amara—a radiant orb pulsating with energy, casting shadows that danced along the walls.

Azad was entranced by its beauty, his heart racing as he took a step closer. But as he reached for the orb, a deafening roar echoed through the chamber. The walls shook, and the very ground beneath them trembled. From the shadows emerged a figure, cloaked in darkness, with eyes that glimmered like stars. It was a guardian of Sayal, an ancient being that had protected the kingdom for millennia.

"You dare to trespass in this sacred space?" the guardian's voice boomed, echoing with the weight of ages. "You seek to claim what does not belong to you, and for that, you shall pay the price."

Azad, fueled by arrogance, drew his sword, but the guardian raised a hand, and the air crackled with power. "You do not understand the forces you toy with. The Light of Amara is not a weapon to be wielded; it is a force of balance. Those who seek to control it shall be met with the wrath of the ancient gods."

Azad's bravado faltered as the guardian's words sank in. He realized that he was not merely facing a man; he was challenging an entity older than time itself. The aura of the guardian was overwhelming, suffocating his resolve, and in that moment, he understood the futility of his ambition.

Yet, desperation drove him forward. "I will not be denied!" he shouted, lunging at the guardian. But in an instant, the guardian vanished, and Azad found himself surrounded by shadows that seemed to close in around him.

The soldiers who had followed Azad into the temple began to scream as the shadows enveloped them. One by one, they were consumed by the darkness, their cries echoing in the chamber. Azad's heart raced as he felt the shadows clawing at his own soul, dragging him down into an abyss of despair.

As Azad Khan stood amidst the chaos, a realization struck him: his ambition had brought him to this cursed place, but it was his arrogance that had sealed his fate. The guardian had warned him, yet he had refused to heed the call of reason. The shadows tightened their grip, and he could feel the weight of countless souls pressing upon him, their anger and despair mingling with his own.

With every fiber of his being, he fought against the darkness, struggling to escape the inevitable. But it was futile; the very land he had sought to conquer had risen against him. The whispers of the Sayalite ancestors filled his mind, drowning out his thoughts, wrapping him in their sorrow and rage. He fell to his knees, realizing too late that true power was not something that could be seized; it was a responsibility, a burden that required respect and reverence.

In his final moments, as the shadows consumed him, Azad's mind flashed back to the tales of his childhood—the legends of the demigods, the sacred pacts, and the ancient powers that ruled the world. He had longed to become a god, but the true essence of divinity lay not in domination, but in harmony.

The guardian reappeared, standing tall amidst the swirling shadows, a look of sorrow etched upon its ethereal face. "You sought to take what was never yours," it spoke softly, the power of its voice resonating through the chamber. "But know this: every action has its consequence, and the legacy you leave will echo through the ages."

With those final words, the guardian raised its hand, and in an instant, the darkness engulfed Azad. The temple trembled, and the ground shook as the ancient powers reasserted their dominion over the land. In a blinding flash of light, Azad Khan and his army were erased from existence, their ambition extinguished like a flame in the wind.

In the years that followed, the legend of Azad Khan transformed into a cautionary tale passed down through generations. The people of Sayal spoke of the shadowy invader who sought to claim their sacred land, only to be consumed by the very darkness he had unleashed. The story became a testament to the balance between ambition and respect for the forces that govern existence.

The ruins of the temple remained, a silent witness to the recklessness of man and the eternal guardianship of the Sayalite ancestors. It became a pilgrimage site for those seeking wisdom and a reminder of the dangers of hubris. Travelers from far and wide came to stand before the sacred site, paying homage to the ancient spirits that still lingered in the shadows.

As the years turned into centuries, the echoes of Azad Khan's ambition faded, but the lessons learned from his downfall remained etched in the collective memory of the land. The Light of Amara continued to shine brightly, a beacon of hope for those who sought to understand the true nature of power.

In the end, Azad Khan became a part of the very legends he had sought to conquer—a specter in the annals of history, a name whispered in reverence and caution, a reminder of the delicate balance between ambition and the sacred guardianship of the forces that shape our world.

Present Time:

The scorching heat of May 2021... The world was still reeling from the devastation of the COVID-19 pandemic. A Sky Air Airlines flight from London was soon to land at Delhi Airport.

Meanwhile, in a small flat in Old Delhi, a hacker's den buzzed with activity—computers, laptops, and an elaborate setup filled the room.

The hacker's name was Usman Qureshi. Usman was sleeping on his bed when suddenly, alert notifications started blaring from his smartphone, laptop, preview monitors, and desktop. A passenger's passport, which Usman had marked for surveillance,

had triggered the alerts. The passport was flagged so that whenever its owner traveled anywhere in the country or the world, Usman would be notified.

Awakening from his deep sleep, Usman realised that the passport's owner was about to land in Delhi from London.

Usman immediately grabbed his mobile and called his boss, Acharya.

Usman (very excited):
"Boss... Boss, you won't believe what I've found!"

(On the other side of the phone...)

The biggest gangsters of the country and the world were gathered in front of the most powerful person of India i.e. Acharya was in his office and their meeting was going on, but Acharya was talking on the phone with his hacker Osman.

Acharya (in a serious tone):
"You're speaking as if you've just stumbled upon the Kohinoor diamond... Remember, son, the punishment for wasting my time is severe."

Usman (on the other end of the phone):
"Sir... the special guest you and your family have been waiting for these past 75 years... she's finally returning to India. Yes, Robert Richardson's granddaughter is coming back to India."

The room is dimly lit, filled with an air of secrecy. ACHARYA, a formidable figure in his mid-60s, sits at the head of a long table surrounded by high-profile gangsters. Their faces are shrouded in shadows, emphasizing the clandestine nature of the gathering.

Acharya (intently):
"Usman, you'd better not be playing games with me. This information is too valuable, so if you're joking, think carefully before you speak."

Usman (over the phone, sincere):
"I swear, Acharya, this is no joke. The granddaughter of Robert Richardson, the one you've been searching for, is on her way to India."

Acharya leans back in his chair, a sinister smile forming on his lips.

Acharya (to his associates):
"Gentlemen, it seems our long-awaited guest has finally decided to grace us with her presence. Get ready—our wait is over."

BACK TO:

Usman feverishly works on his computer, digging deeper into the passport details. He uncovers a series of encrypted messages indicating a larger conspiracy surrounding the Richardson family.

Usman (on the phone):
"Boss, there's something more. I intercepted

encrypted messages related to the Richardson family. It's not just a reunion; it's a setup."

Acharya (over the phone, focused):
"Bring me everything you've got, Usman. We'll make sure this reunion is one they'll never forget."

Usman continues to unravel the mystery, unaware of the dangerous game he's entangled in.

CUT TO:

The Sky Air Airlines flight from London lands. The anticipation in the air is palpable as passengers disembark.

Flashback -

1 Year ago 2020 - London

Miles away from India, a 102-year-old man was lying on a bed in a Big Bunglow in London city, counting his last breaths. Even the top doctors of London gave up after seeing his condition.

Family members of Richardson Family were all gathered and waiting for the response of the doctors in the hope that maybe now they would get to hear some good news, the name of that old man was Mr. Robertson Richards, a very famous industrialist of London, the doctors came out. Said that they wanted to meet Professor Robertson's granddaughter Jessica. What the doctors came to know about Jessica was that

Jessica was actually a British citizen of Indian origin, who was the granddaughter of Robertson, that is, a proud heir of his huge business empire. Actually, Jessica's grandfather was an Englishman, he was married to an Indian, that is why she is half English and half Indian.

Doctor (worried):
"The condition of your grandfather is beyond our understanding. As you know, he has been suffering from half-body paralysis for many years. At over 100 years old, most bodily functions gradually cease, but something unusual is happening with your grandfather. I'm struggling to explain this... how can I put it?"

Jessica:
"What's happening to him? Are you saying it's impossible to save him now? Are you considering turning off his life support?"

Doctor (worried):
"Jessica, listen carefully. You might think I'm crazy, but your grandfather's organs are stable. Even if we remove the life support, his heart continues to beat, and his organs function as if they're in a much younger body. It's as if... he's immortal. Despite his weakened state and paralysis, his organs are functioning normally. At his age, his body should be failing, but something is preventing his death."

Jessica (sarcastic):
"Are you all professional doctors? Do you

actually know what you're saying? Are you sure you're not a madman? A 100-year-old man with half his body paralysed, whose organs still work like a young man's, and you can't even kill him if you tried? Why? Since he's immortal, should he quit medicine and start scripting for Avengers?"

Doctor (smiling):
"I understand how unbelievable this sounds, Jessica. However, we have conducted numerous tests and consulted with experts worldwide, and the conclusion remains the same. Your grandfather's condition is indeed extraordinary and beyond our medical understanding. It's not immortality in the traditional sense, but his body seems to defy the usual ageing process and expected organ decline."

Jessica (sarcastic):
"So, what's the plan, Doctor? Are we going to witness a medical miracle or send him to the next Avengers movie?"

Doctor (laughing):
"I assure you, Jessica, this isn't a movie plot. We're in uncharted territory here. We'll continue to monitor his condition, provide comfort, and explore any possible avenues for

alleviating his suffering. But we must be realistic about the challenges we face."

Jessica (serious):
"I appreciate your honesty, Doctor. It's just difficult to accept that my grandfather is in such a unique situation. What can we do to make him more comfortable?"

Doctor:
"We'll work closely with your family to manage his pain and ensure he receives the best care possible. We're also reaching out to medical researchers and specialists who might have insights into conditions like his. It's a delicate situation, but we're committed to doing everything we can."

Jessica (nodding):
"Alright, Doctor. Let's focus on making him as comfortable as possible. And who knows, maybe someday medical science will catch up with his uniqueness."

The doctor and Jessica continue their conversation, discussing the options available for Mr. Robertson Richards, the 102-year-old man with an extraordinary condition that defies medical explanation.

Then Jessica gets a call from her elderly grandfather.

Walking slowly, Jessica enters her grandfather's room. There she sees her grandfather with countless stars on his body and an oxygen mask on his mouth.

Slowly Robertson removes the mask from his mouth and looks at Jessica and says

Robertson - (UPSET)

You are finding my condition funny, look at me. .....I can't die even if I fucking want to

Jessica - (Apologetic)

No no GrandPa, I was telling this to those doctors. .. I. ...I had no intention of making fun of you

Robertson -

Do you think that my condition looks like a Hollywood science fiction movie, whatever has happened to me today, I am the only one responsible for it, the trouble which I had brought with me 76 years ago considering it a blessing, has made me Even after giving everything, everything was taken away from me, people think immortality is a blessing. .... No, not at all, this is a curse that will probably keep me alive till the end of time. ....and finally he took away my family from me too

Jessica -

Grandfather, what curse are you talking about? And how did you get into such a condition, mom and dad all died due to this curse?

Robertson said to Jessica in a very serious tone -

Robertson -

listen carefully. ....It all started from India

Robertson takes a deep breath before continuing his story.

Robertson - It was back in 1948, just after the independence of India. I was an adventurous young man, and the stories of mystical lands and ancient curses fascinated me. I embarked on a journey to explore the hidden corners of India, seeking the secrets that were said to be *buried within its rich history.*

During my travels, I encountered a wise old sage in a remote village. He spoke of a sacred artifact, a talisman that was said to grant immortality. The idea of living forever was alluring, and I, blinded by my youthful arrogance, decided to seek out this artifact. The sage warned me of the consequences, but I paid no heed.

After months of searching, I finally found the artifact hidden deep within an ancient temple. It was a small, ornate box with intricate carvings. The sage's warnings echoed in my mind, but the temptation was too strong. I opened the box, and a blinding light enveloped me.

The year is 1990,In March 1990, a village in India... On one side, the entire village was immersed in celebrations on the occasion of Syal Gaon Mahashivratri, while on the other side

the lush forests of Sayal village whisper with the winds of change as India inches towards *the Globalisation Amidst the verdant foliage, a British police officer, **CAPTAIN ROBERTSON**, rides his horse deep into the heart of the jungle.*

CUT TO:

Archelogist Robertson, guided by an inexplicable force, stumbles upon the ruins of a mysterious temple. Covered in vines and hidden from the prying eyes of the world, the temple emanates an aura of ancient secrets.

CUT TO:

Captain Robertson, holding a torch, cautiously steps inside the dilapidated temple. The air is thick with a sense of foreboding, and the flickering torchlight casts eerie shadows on the crumbling walls.

As he ventures deeper, the temple reveals a hidden chamber adorned with a breathtaking statue of a goddess. The beauty of the sculpture captivates him, and he becomes entranced by its ethereal allure.

Suddenly, Captain Robertson notices a concealed tunnel leading further into the temple. Driven by curiosity, he decides to explore the enigmatic passage.

CUT TO:

Captain Robertson ventures into the depths of the temple, and what he encounters defies all logic. The tunnel unfolds into a cavernous space, adorned with ancient symbols and artifacts that seem to tell tales of a bygone era.

As he delves deeper, the air becomes charged with an otherworldly energy. Captain Robertson feels a presence, an awareness that transcends time itself. The mysterious atmosphere envelopes him, and he becomes acutely aware of an existence beyond his understanding.

Suddenly, a bone-chilling scream echoes through the temple, piercing the silence of the jungle. Captain Robertson, his face drained of color, emerges from the depths in a state of terror. His incoherent ramblings hint at an encounter with an unimaginable force within the temple.

CUT TO:

Captain Robertson, disheveled and shaken, stumbles out of the temple. The once tranquil forest now shudders with an unsettling energy. The village, unaware of the unearthly *events, remains wrapped in the cloak of darkness as Captain Robertson's scream echoes through the night.*

From that moment on, my life changed. I stopped aging, and I became impervious to illness or injury. At first, I reveled in my newfound immortality, but as time passed, I realized the true nature of the curse. I watched my loved ones age and wither away while I remained unchanged.

Jessica -

Grandfather, but how did this curse take them away?

Robertson -

The artifact demanded a price for its gift. It fed on the life force of those around me. The longer I lived, the more it consumed. My family, my friends – they all fell victim to the curse. The more I loved, the more the artifact took from me. I'm left with the burden of endless years, surrounded by the ghosts of the past.

Jessica -

Grandfather, we need to find a way to break this curse, to free you from this suffering.

Robertson -

It's too late, Jessica. The only way to break the curse is to destroy the artifact, but its location remains unknown. I've spent decades searching, but to no avail. Now, I'm trapped in this immortal existence, haunted by the consequences of my own foolishness.

Jessica, overwhelmed with emotion, reaches out and holds her grandfather's hand.

Jessica - We will find a way, Grandfather. I won't let you face this alone.

As Jessica promises to help her grandfather, a sense of determination fills the room, setting the stage for a new chapter in their lives, as they embark on a quest to unravel the mysteries of the artifact and break the ancient curse.

But Grandpa, what is this Yakshini?

FADE OUT.

Robertson Narrates -

This story begins with a legend. ,

Goddess Adi Shakti, mother of the endless universe and creator of millions of gods and goddesses.But one of her creations is such that it is neither described in any Purana nor in any scripture.

In the quiet village of Sayal, nestled amidst rolling hills and lush greenery, an ancient temple stood as a testament to a forgotten goddess—Yakshini. Legends whispered of her once-beautiful form, crafted from molten gold by the hands of the mighty Goddess Adishakti. However, the tale took a tragic turn as Yakshini's insatiable greed led her to theft and rebellion against her divine creator.

The longing for Yakshini's beauty spread like wildfire across the universe, captivating the hearts of gods, humans, and demons alike. Yet, her desire for the infinite gold of heaven and the boundless energy of Goddess Adishakti transformed into a destructive greed. In her audacious pursuit, Yakshini stole heavenly gold at her whim.

However, when she dared to covet the limitless energy of Adishakti herself, disaster struck. The divine energy proved too potent for the golden Yakshini, and half her body was consumed by its searing heat. Goddess Adishakti, who had once created Yakshini as a beacon of beauty and love, now faced no choice but to end her creation's existence.

Kicked out from the heavens, Yakshini became a symbol of ugliness and poverty, cursed by the very goddess who had birthed her. Her name was erased from scriptures, her tales forgotten, and her image shrouded in anonymity.

Yet, as time flowed like a river, civilizations rose and fell, and the village of Sayal found itself steeped in the whims of lustful and greedy humans. They established a temple for the forgotten Yakshini, ignorant of the wrath they were inviting upon themselves.

The anger of Goddess Adishakti loomed over the skies of Sayal village, casting shadows on its landscape. The village, once bathed in the warmth of sunlight, now faced perpetual darkness. The people suffered under the weight of the curse, their lives plagued by misfortune and hardship.

As the temple of Yakshini stood as a reminder of humanity's folly, the villagers of Sayal found themselves trapped in a never-ending cycle of Curse . The once-forgotten goddess, cursed and abandoned, had found a new home in the shadows of a village that dared to defy the divine order. The sunlight, a distant memory, seemed forever out of reach for the people of Sayal.

FADE IN:

THREE
2020

JULY 2021

The tranquil village of Sayal, surrounded by nature, struggles under the weight of a global lockdown. The financial distress hits hard on Vijay Pandey, a talented Sculpture Artist residing in the village.

Vijay, surrounded by his sculptures, receives no assignments due to the lockdown. Frustration brews, leading to constant arguments with his wife, Sujatha. The unpaid school fees for their son, Bablu/Mahesh, add to the mounting stress.

VIJAY

(Talking to a client on the phone, frustrated)

"Sir, what are you saying? What do you mean you can't make the payment because of the lockdown? I made all these sculptures just on your request, sir. I borrowed money from the market specifically for this project. Please try to understand my situation, sir. I'm drowning in debt, and I desperately need the money. Why aren't you understanding my predicament?"

Before he could finish his sentence, Vijay's client disconnected the call.

Vijay (Talking to himself)

"This lockdown has turned me into a beggar. Damn it!

Why didn't this coronavirus affect me?
If I had to endure a life of debt and starvation, it would've been better to just die."

He seeks solace in loans from friends, but the struggle intensifies.

Vijay was calling all his friends and clients around the world one by one to get some financial help from them but he was unable to do so, but there his husband Sujata comes to his workshop, but here he is in tension and stress. Drowned Vijay was walking from here to there in the workshop with a cigarette in one hand and checking messages on his phone.

Then Sujata, Vijay's wife, comes inside the room and says
Sujata
"Vijay, can you hear me? ...The household supplies are on the verge of running out."
Vijay
"Yes, I'll see what I can do."
Sujata
"And don't forget, Shubham's school fees are due soon."
Vijay (puffing a cigarette)
"Hmm."
Sujata
"Vijay... Vijay?"
Vijay (frustrated, shouting)
"For God's sake, I can't do anything right now! Don't you understand? All my orders have been cancelled, I have no work at the moment. I've called ten people since morning, I owe money to fifty people, and I need to collect from a hundred, but no one is picking up their bloody phone! What do you expect me to do?"
Sujata
"Raising your voice won't solve anything, Vijay. Getting angry isn't going to bring money into this house, alright? And what

about that Delhi event you were talking about? You said it was going to bring in a lot of money. What happened to that? You were so confident, saying there would be a good payout. What happened?"

Vijay

"The Delhi Cultural Art Exhibition was cancelled because of the second wave of Covid. I can't do anything about it. No one's even answering my calls. Tell me, what should I do now? Should I rob a bank to meet your expectations?"

Saying this, Vijay storms out of the room, and Sujata angrily shouts after him:

Sujata

"If you can't support a family, why did you get married? I would have been better off dying single than marrying a beggar like you!"

Vijay ignores his wife's words and leaves the place angrily.

Vijay came out of his house in an angry state. He was wandering on the streets of his locality while smoking a cigarette when he saw his old friend Rajan.When vijay was roaming outside of his house , he

encounters his old friend, Rajan.

Rajan

"Oi, Vijay!"

Vijay was passing by, puffing on a cigarette, lost in his thoughts, so he didn't hear his old friend Rajan's call. But Rajan called out to him again.

Vijay

"Oh, Rajan... How are you, mate? Sorry, I didn't see you there. How have you been?"

Rajan

"I'm good, mate. I recently started a gold showroom."

Vijay
"Really? Your business is doing well even during this recession?"
Rajan
"Yeah, mate, it's going great. Even during the recession, the income's been good. I actually bought a Mercedes-Benz just a little while ago."

As he said this, Rajan pointed towards his car parked in the distance.
Vijay
"That's impressive, mate. Just like your name suggests, you're living like a king."
Rajan
"Forget about me, mate. Tell me, how's your sculpture business doing?"

After a brief silence, Vijay replied in a heavy, emotional voice:
Vijay
"It's all over."
Cut to - Rajan's Home
Both Rajan and Vijay were drinking alcohol while sitting in Rajan's big bungalow, where Vijay told him about his financial crisis and how he was facing financial crisis due to the sudden cancellation of a big cultural event in Delhi.
Rajan (worried):
"This is really bad, mate."
Vijay (replied while drinking):
"Hmmm... You're right, it's terrible." (Takes a sip of whisky)
"How am I supposed to pay off a 7 lakh debt? I have no idea. And to top it off, my wife's father cursed me by marrying me off to an illiterate, unlucky woman. She neither earns a living nor lets her husband live in peace. But tell me, how are you making so much money, mate? I can't wrap my head around it. You're doing well even in this recession."

Rajan:
"It's nothing like that, mate."
Vijay:
"Come on, spill it... Did you stumble upon Aladdin's lamp? How are you making so much money and achieving such success? Six months ago, you were borrowing money from me. Now, how have you got so much cash?"
Rajan:
"Let's just say I did find something like Aladdin's lamp. But if I tell you, you'll laugh at me and say I'm making up stories."
Vijay:
"Mate, a drowning man will cling to straws. Maybe if I listen to you, I might find a way out. Right now, if I could, I'd rob a bank."
Rajan:
"So, you're saying you'd do anything?"
Vijay:
"Anything..."
Rajan:
"Only those who know how to dive deep into the sea of dangers and pull others down with them can live a life of luxury. If you want to awaken your dormant fate... get ready to take a risk."
Rajan whispers:
"Yakshini Temple's soil."
Vijay (laughs):
"Soil? What do you want me to do? Make another sculpture out of it? When did you start writing poetry, mate?"
Rajan (smiles):
"I knew you'd laugh if I told you my secret... No worries, mate. Keep laughing, and the future will keep making you cry."
Putting down the wine glass, Vijay responds to his friend, now feeling embarrassed.

Vijay:

"Hey, hey, mate, why are you getting so worked up? Come on, tell me… What's the secret behind your wealth, mate?"

Rajan:

"Listen… Just outside our town, deep within that reserve forest, there's a temple that's over 300 years old. It's completely abandoned, but the soil from that temple can turn the poorest beggar into a wealthy man. They say the gold inside the temple is infinite and never runs out."

Vijay listens attentively to his friend, but suddenly his expression changes. First, he smiles, then his face shows embarrassment.

Vijay (skeptical):

"This superstition of yours won't pay off my debts. These stories sound good to listen to, but practically, they don't hold any weight."

Rajan:

"Look, mate, you already have a 7 lakh debt hanging over your head. Tell me, do you have any other way out?"

Despite his disbelief, Vijay, even under the influence of alcohol, replies seriously.

Vijay (serious tone):

"Rajan, mate, the situation I'm in right now, struggling with this financial crisis… it's no joke. And you're mocking me with all this talk of soil and temples?"

Vijay takes the last sip of wine, sets down the glass, and says:

Vijay (embarrassed):

"Thanks for wasting my precious time."

Vijay starts to leave, but Rajan calls out from behind.

Rajan:

"The Sultan of Delhi didn't believe in this either…"

Vijay stops in his tracks.

Rajan:

"In 1724... When the Sultan sitting on Delhi's throne tried to loot this part of India... overnight, the small king of Sayal wiped out the Sultan's 100,000-strong army. Ever wondered how a small king managed to do that? Because he, too, sought help from that same temple, the one whose soil I now possess. He worshipped the same goddess who isn't worshipped anywhere else... If a mighty king could do this to save his kingdom, then what's stopping us common folk?"

Vijay:

"Your superstition can't clear my debt."

Rajan:

"I've paid off my debts with what you call superstition. Whether any god listens to your prayers or not... that temple's goddess will definitely hear your call, just like she heard that king's 300 years ago."

Saying this, Rajan hands Vijay a wad of Rs 25,000 notes.

Rajan:

"Take this money. I know you're in desperate need right now. No need to pay it back."

Though Vijay was sceptical, his financial crisis forced him to accept the money from Rajan. He left the place, but as he walked along the deserted streets of Sayal, Rajan's words echoed in his mind. He still didn't want to believe them, but he had no other options.

Walking alone on the quiet streets, Vijay was torn between disbelief and desperation. Despite his doubts, he decides to visit the temple.

CUT TO - Next Morning

Acharya's goons, sent by him, were lying in wait outside the airport, ready to kidnap Jessica as soon as she stepped out. Although Jessica belonged to a wealthy and noble family in London, she was originally from India. She wanted to keep her arrival a secret, as she needed to remain discreet about her mission. However, little did she know that many were already waiting for her.

In the airport parking lot, Acharya's trusted man, Bakshi, was working under the guidance of Acharya's hacker, Osman. Bakshi spoke to Osman on the phone.

Bakshi (on the phone):
"Brother, her flight has landed, but she hasn't come out yet. She's probably collecting her luggage from the belt."

Osman (on the other end):
"As soon as she leaves the airport in her car, start following her. But don't do anything until her car stops at the first traffic signal. That's when you should kidnap her."

Bakshi:
"But, Osman Bhai, what about the CCTV cameras here?"

Osman:
"I'll hack them from here and turn them off, but remember, you'll only have 3 minutes after I do. That's the window you'll have to abduct her using our secret route."

Bakshi:
"Understood, Bhai."

Osman:
"There's no room for mistakes. The traffic signal where her car will stop is the least crowded. No errors, got it?"

Bakshi:
"Don't worry, Bhai... I'll get the job done. Just let that English madam step out of the airport."

These people were talking among themselves when Bashi's companion informed him that Jessica had left the airport and took a taxi from there. As soon as Jessica's car reached outside the airport, he secretly stopped Jessica's car. As soon as Osman hacked the signal at which Jessica's car was stopped, those goons started firing bullets at Jessica's car so that she could not run away from there. Seeing all this, Jessica gets nervous and says

jessica (panic)

*- What the fu*k? What's happening?*

Before she could understand anything, her driver gets shot and forcibly drags her out of the car. Bakshi takes her with him to the container in front of him, loads her in that container truck, starts it and runs away from there with his friends. Goes on the secret route he has decided on

Seeing that a man was so brutally shot and killed in front of Jessica's eyes, she became very scared, she didn't even know what was going to happen next, Jessica, sitting inside the container, started beating her hands here and there. Did

Jessica -

Is there anyone? Please help. ,

The driver of the container had a different plan but then

The man, wearing a mask and hiding his face, took out his mobile and redialed the last dialed number of the caller.

Bakshi was happy because his plan was successfully executed without any hindrance, but suddenly the tires of his and his accompanying cars were fired from snipers and there was a huge explosion due to which all the three cars accompanying Bakshi stopped at the same place.

The driver of the container was actually a loyal man of the Richardson company who had secretly come to take Jessica away safely, while Bakshi and him kept staring at him and the container driver took Jessica away from there.

That container and its driver had escaped from the clutches of Bakshi and his goons, here that container had reached a safe house outside Delhi, Jessica still did not realize that she had been saved, that safe of that container. As soon as they reached the house, the container was opened. Jessica started shouting and making noise. She still felt that she had been kidnapped by

Bakshi's goons.

Jessica - Somebody Please Help

The man moved towards Jessica with a knife in his hands. Seeing this, Jessica was completely scared, she thought that he had come to kill.

Jessica (scared)

No no no please don't kill me..... no

But that person cut Jessica's rope with the same knife.

Jessica was surprised to see this

The unknown person introduced himself to Jessica and said

Viren -

Don't worry Jessica madam, you are safe now, my name is Viren. .... Their plan was to kidnap you from the airport but I took you out at the right time.

(Taking out the mobile from his pocket and dialing a number, he said while placing the mobile in Jessica's hands)

Viren -

Ye Lo Baat karo insey

Jessica nervously took the phone from his hand.

Jessica - (Nervous)

Hello........

Jessica's manager on the other end of the phone is from London.

George - (angry)

Jessica why did you come to India

Jessica -

George. ....What is all this happening with me, a man shot my driver in broad daylight in front of me, in front of me, in a crowded road, we have to go to the police, please call someone for help. Need to inform someone

Viren -

Insab ka koi fayada nahi madam, ye log bahut powerful log hai,inkey khilaaf na koi witness hoga naa hii cctv recording

George -

I had a feeling that something like this was going to happen, that's why I had already informed Viren, but these people are very powerful people, at this time no one can save you in the whole of India, that is why it is better to return as soon as possible. take a flight back here to london

Jessica said taking a deep breath

Jessica - (in a deep voice)

For me now all this is one way, there is no option for me to go back now. ....

To free Grand Paa, I will have to find the Yakshini temple. ,

I have no other option

George -

Jessica, they have been searching for you and your entire family for the last many years, Acharya is thirsty for your blood, they hold only you and your grandfather responsible for their current condition, your grandfather felt that Curse. ....It has wreaked havoc on his family too. ....Either come back or else. ,

Viren -

I can help you.

On one hand, Jessica, with the help of Viren, was moving towards the small village of Assam by road in an SUV car while avoiding Acharya and his people.

One by one, Jessica and Viren were moving towards Assam, somehow crossing all the state borders between Delhi and Assam.

Angered by the failure of his people, Acharya's temper was rising.

Bakshi and his men were following Osman with folded hands to apologize for their failure because due to their stupidity and carelessness someone else rescued Jessica from them.

The scene opens with VIJAY driving his car through the dark and desolate streets of Sayal. The night is eerily quiet, with only the sound of his car's engine humming through the silence. The tension is palpable as Vijay's face reflects a mix of determination and fear. The trees along the road sway slightly as if warning him of what lies ahead.

Suddenly, the radio in Vijay's car crackles to life, interrupting the tense silence.

Radio Announcer (worried voice): "Sorry for the interruption, but we've just received an urgent weather update. A massive cyclone is rapidly approaching Assam, and due to this, a state-wide high alert has been issued. We advise everyone to stay away from coastal areas and remain indoors tonight. Please stock up on emergency supplies for the next two days if you haven't already."

The radio crackles again before falling silent. Vijay glances at the radio, his grip on the steering wheel tightening. The warning lingers in the air, but he continues driving towards the reserve forest, undeterred by the announcement.

The camera shifts to a wide shot, showing the empty, winding road leading into the dense forest. The moonlight barely penetrates the thick canopy of trees, casting long, ominous shadows on the road ahead. The sound of the wind picking up can be heard faintly in the background, hinting at the approaching storm.

As Vijay drives deeper into the forest, the sense of isolation grows stronger. The trees close in around him, and the road becomes narrower. The only light comes from his car's headlights, which cut through the darkness like a knife.

Vijay's thoughts race as he recalls Rajan's words about the temple and the mysterious soil. Doubt and skepticism still cloud his mind, but desperation pushes him forward. He knows this might be his last chance to save himself from his crushing debt.

Suddenly, the car radio crackles to life again, but this time, the signal is faint and distorted. Vijay can barely make out the voice of the announcer, but the warning about the cyclone is clear.

Radio Announcer (distorted): "...dangerous cyclone... take shelter immediately..."

Vijay's grip tightened on the steering wheel as he drove with grim determination, the storm outside escalating in ferocity. The radio's urgent warning barely pierced through the cacophony of howling winds and torrential rain lashing against his car. He could barely see beyond the windshield, which was streaked with heavy rain and illuminated by sporadic flashes of lightning. Each thunderclap resonated like a drumbeat in the oppressive darkness that enveloped him.

The forest loomed ahead, its shadowy depths barely discernible through the tempest. Vijay knew the reserve forest was his destination, but the weather seemed to conspire against him, each gust of wind threatening to wrench control from his hands. The trees were whipping violently in the storm, their branches clawing at the sky as if trying to reach through the chaos above. Vijay's face, illuminated intermittently by the jagged flashes of lightning, was etched with unwavering resolve. He was driven by an unshakable determination, though the forest promised both peril and mystery.

The camera captures a close-up of Vijay's face, drenched in sweat and rain, his eyes narrowing against the storm's fury. The relentless storm roared like a beast, its howling wind mixing with the deep, foreboding rumble of thunder. Vijay's breath came out in short, steamy bursts, and his knuckles were white as he pressed the accelerator, pushing through the storm towards the unknown heart of the forest.

Cut to black.

Meanwhile, miles away, Viren and Jessica were navigating their way through the rugged terrain of Assam, the state borders just behind them. Their car was similarly battered by the worsening weather, and the same ominous radio broadcast had reached them too. The air inside the vehicle was tense, fraught with the unease brought on by the encroaching storm. Jessica, who had been driving in silence, seemed detached from the turmoil around her, her eyes fixed on the dark, rain-slicked road ahead. The unsettling quiet in the car was punctuated only by the low, constant murmur of the radio.

Viren, noticing Jessica's unusual silence and the pallor of her face illuminated by the dashboard lights, was growing increasingly concerned. He reached out, placing a hand gently on her shoulder.

FOUR
TEMPLE OF YAKSHINI

Viren:

"Oh, dear God! Of all times, the weather had to worsen now?"

He watched as Jessica remained unresponsive, her silence unnerving. Viren's worry deepened as he noticed her fixation, her eyes darting occasionally as though she were hearing something beyond the ordinary. He could not fathom what was troubling her, but her behavior suggested that something was amiss.

Viren:

"Miss Jessica... are you alright?"

His voice, soft but concerned, barely penetrated the heavy atmosphere of the car. Jessica appeared startled, as if jolted from a trance. Her eyes blinked rapidly, and she seemed to come back to herself, the whispers in her ears abruptly falling silent. Viren, now fully alarmed, brought the car to a halt on the side of the road, the engine rumbling softly against the storm's backdrop.

Viren:

"What's the matter? Are you okay? What happened to you?"

Jessica:

"No, no, I'm fine. Perhaps it's just fatigue."
Viren:
"Let's do something—there's a small café nearby. Let's stop for some tea; it might help you feel better. Maybe you're just tired, and that's why this is happening."

Jessica, placing her hand over her mouth as if to stifle a tremor, nodded. Her attempt at reassurance did little to quell Viren's growing apprehension. The unease she felt was palpable, and the storm outside seemed to echo her internal turmoil.
Jessica:
"Yes, I'm fine. Perhaps it's just the exhaustion that's making me feel so strange."

They decided to stop at a roadside dhaba, the flickering lights of the small establishment a beacon in the storm. As they exited the car, the wind buffeted them with cold, wet blasts. The café was a humble, rustic structure, its wooden sign creaking ominously in the gale. Stepping inside, the warmth and the faint, comforting aroma of tea provided a brief respite from the relentless storm.

The dhaba was sparsely populated, the few patrons huddled in their seats, their faces drawn with fatigue and worry. Viren led Jessica to a table near the small, crackling heater, trying to offer her some comfort. As they waited for their tea, the sound of the storm outside seemed to intensify, the wind howling like a banshee against the thin walls of the café.

Viren tried to engage Jessica in conversation, hoping to break the spell of her silence. His attempts to lighten the mood were met with a distant smile from Jessica, who still seemed lost in her thoughts. Her gaze was often distant, her fingers nervously drumming on the table.
Viren:
"You know, sometimes a hot cup of tea can do wonders. It's like a small comfort in the midst of chaos."

Jessica:

"Yes, I suppose so. I think I needed this break."

The storm continued its relentless assault on the world outside, a reminder of the dangers that lay ahead. Jessica's internal struggle remained hidden beneath her composed exterior, but the eerie feeling she had experienced in the car lingered. The whispers and the sounds that had haunted her were not just echoes of the storm; they were the ominous harbingers of something darker yet to come.

As they sipped their tea, the café's warm light offered a temporary reprieve, but the storm's howling winds and the flickering lights cast long shadows across their faces. The unsettling sense of foreboding hung heavily in the air, hinting at the trials and dangers that lay in wait.

Viren:

(Jokingly) Miss Jessica, I insist you try this piping hot tea. After all, if you've come to India and haven't tasted our tea, can you truly say you've experienced *Bharat Darshan*?

Jessica:

(Reluctantly) Hmm.

(Viren realised that whatever had happened over the past few hours had deeply troubled Jessica. He thought perhaps a cup of tea might lighten her mood. As he handed over the tea, he said.)

Viren:

Here you are, Miss Jessica. Have some tea.

(Jessica took the tea and immediately took a sip. Suddenly, she let out a small cry, having not realised how hot it was and burning her mouth.)

Jessica:

(Jokingly) Well, at least the tea has done its job. I've finally had a taste of India.

(Hearing Viren's words, a smile spread across Jessica's face, and she laughed. Seeing her laugh, Viren couldn't help but join in.)

Viren:

Well, at least the tea has managed to give you a taste of India.

Jessica:

The people of your India have welcomed me so warmly since my arrival. I won't be able to forget this hospitality for the rest of my life.

(Then the waiter at the dhaba spoke up.)

Waiter:

*Madam, your true *Bharat Darshan* won't be complete until you've tried our country's *golgappas*. They're so full of flavour... ummm! Once you've tasted them, you'll never forget it.*

(Another customer seated nearby sarcastically chimed in.)

Customer:

*How could anyone forget? After all, if the *pani puri* upsets your stomach, you might just find yourself confined to the toilet for days. And that's not exactly a taste you'd want to remember!*

(Upon hearing this, both Viren and Jessica burst into laughter. Viren then seized the moment to ask Jessica.)

Viren:

Miss Jessica, if you don't mind, may I ask you something?

Jessica:

Yes, of course.

Viren:

Since you arrived in India, so much has happened to you. Many people want to take your life... Yet, you still don't wish to leave, and you continue to search for that small town, Syal... Why is that? Is there a special reason?

Till now Jessica's face, which was full of happiness, had now become indifferent.

Jessica - (in a serious tone)

Some promises and relationships are above life and death, Viren, whatever my grandfather has done for me, no work I have done is anything, for him I can do anything, I can go anywhere.

Viren -

Madam, I will take you to that place, but what should we do from there?

Jessica -

i had a friend over there, he is an archeologist, may be he can help

After wandering in the forest for hours, Vijay was upset and now he was completely tired because Vijay was unable to find the Yakshini temple. In despair, Vijay came and sat near the biggest waterfall of the forest. He was trying to remember Rajan's words and remembered that Rajan had said that

(flashback)

Rajan -

Where your path ends at the biggest waterfall of the forest, the desire to reach Yakshini temple begins from there.

Vijay was trying to concentrate on his mind when suddenly his foot slips and he falls straight towards the waterfall inside the river, somehow Vijay controlled himself and then he saw a crocodile. Seeing the crocodile, VIJAY felt bad. kind of scared But that crocodile was actually a baby crocodile and Vijay was shocked to see it.

But that crocodile did not do anything to Vijay, he silently turned towards the waterfall and walked towards the waterfall and slowly Vijay also started following him.

Because Vijay knew that such crocodiles are not actually found in India and this is the kind of crocodile which shows people the way to the Yakshini temple, Vijay came and saw it, he immediately cut the branches of the trees nearby and killed them. built like a boat

And with a torch in his hand, Vijay started chasing the crocodile in his wooden boat, the crocodile passed through the waterfall and crossed it.

As soon as VIJAY crossed the waterfall, he saw darkness inside the cave and the abode of bats. Seeing this, Vijay got scared for a minute. Looking at some puzzles written in Sanskrit on the walls of the cave, he saw VIJAY Vijay tried to understand, he had brought with him a diary with Sanskrit to Hindu translation kept in his bag, after reading which he could only understand that the direction of the temple he was looking for was in the tunnels inside the cave, Vijay saw that There are 3 tunnels in front of him, but looking at the marks, Vijay reached ahead of him, the path of two of the 3 tunnels was in two different directions, but the path of the middle tunnel was covered with an old and dusty idol of Yakshini, seeing this Vijay said

Vijay-

"Blimey, no idea which goddess's temple this is, and how on earth did Rajan find his way here!"

As he muttered this, Vijay had just placed his hand on the goddess's idol when suddenly, he felt the ground beneath him shake within the cave.

CUT TO-

On the other hand, VIJAY touched the dusty idol of Yakshini and on the other hand, Jessica suddenly felt a shock, the shock was so strong that suddenly the glass of tea slipped from Jessica's hand and fell on the ground.

Seeing this, Viren came running to Jessica and other people from the restaurant came to help her. Seeing Jessica's condition, people thought that Jessica was probably having an epileptic attack.

cut to -

Here inside the cave

And the ground at the place where he was standing suddenly cracked and Vijay started falling down very fast, in fact it was the only way to reach the secret temple of Yakshini below where Vijay was standing.

While somehow falling through the tunnel, he reached the end of a deep tunnel and fell on the ground,

Vijay Didn't realise but now he was at the temple of Yakshini

there was darkness all around, Vijay then came to one place and fell, Vijay had injuries at various places on his body but he did not understand anything. He was coming and where did he actually reach?

On the other hand, Jessica had stopped suffering from epileptic seizures.

Seeing Jessica's condition, Viren got nervous and as soon as Jessica recovered, he asked

Viren:

"Jessica, you... this, this episode you're having, has it been with you since childhood? Do you suffer from epilepsy?"

***Jessica** (managing her breath):*

"No, Viren... Ever since I entered Assam, all of this started happening to me. I don't even know what it was or what suddenly came over me, but the closer I got to Sayal town, the stranger I felt, as if I was connected to something. It's like someone is whispering in my ears... Someone, somewhere, is trying to tell me something."

***Viren** (out of curiosity):*

"Oh, when you were having these episodes, did you see anything? Anything blurry or unclear before your eyes?"

Jessica remembered again and saw a blurry scene before her eyes, a dark cave lit only by torches and a huge 20 feet statue.

cut to -

Vijay was somehow controlling himself while dragging his body full of injuries and pain inside the cave, he saw only deep darkness all around him. Vijay lit a torch with broken pieces of wood and the scene then appeared before his eyes. Vijay was stunned to see that he came.What Vijay saw before his eyes was beyond imagination.Inside, he discovers a mesmerizing statue of Yakshini, radiating an otherworldly beauty. The atmosphere is charged with an eerie energy.

Vijay stands before the Yakshini statue, captivated by its intricate details. The curves and glow on her face draw him in. Suddenly, a distant scream breaks the silence, causing Vijay to drop his torch. He quickly collects the sacred soil from the temple grounds, loading it into his car.

Vijay

(whispering to himself)

Rajan ne sahi kaha tha.

Just then, a distant scream pierces the silence. Startled, Vijay collects soil from around the statue and hastily leaves.

Vijay was just staring at that beautiful idol of Yakshini when it came to his mind that why not go closer, because of the gold on the surrounding walls, the idol of Yakshini was shining in the light of the torch, it seemed like the saree of the nymphs of heaven. That statue is a mixture of beauty, Vijay was staring at it when he realized that he was not alone in that deserted temple, Vijay started collecting the soil in his bag as per Rajan's advice but he He felt that it was someone's presence and then VIJAY's eyes fell on the jewels fixed on the body of the Yakshini idol, then VIJAY tried to remove one of the many jewels tied on the neck of Yakshini. Here and there, as soon as the idol of Yakshini Vijay touched here and there on the other side

Cut to-

On the other hand, as soon as Jessica was going to sit in the car, her body started trembling once again and this time 100 times more violently than the last time, due to which the people of the nearby dhaba and even Viren got scared seeing this and her body was trembling. It grew so much that Jessica started screaming and as soon as Viren came running to help Jessica, he saw that Jessica's eyes suddenly turned white and her trembling suddenly stopped and then Jessica The eyes turned white and slowly on its own its body started flying in the air, seeing this the people around started running away out of fear and Viren also started moving backwards seeing this, in the midst of a strong storm and terrible lightning thunder. The atmosphere had become even more frightening

And on the other side, in the Yakshini temple, as soon as Vijay pulls out the locket from Yakshini's neck, the sounds of screaming birds start coming from the closed corridors on the other side.

Acharya was sitting in his study room drinking liquor, there was a strong storm and lightning outside and Acharya was drinking pegs of liquor one after the other, then Osman comes to his study room with his tab because he has to wait for 12 hours. After his investigation, he came to know something about Jessica which he came to tell his boss Acharya, Acharya looked at Osman and asked

Acharya -

Kuch Pata Chala ?

Osman -

yes sir look at this

(Showing the tab in his hand to ACHARYA)

Osman -

We traced the last location of her mobile here in Prayagraj and he was seen in the CCTV footage on the highway going from there to Kolkata, but from there he changed his car, it is obvious that they are definitely moving from here towards Kolkata. , because it is the largest international airport of

Eastern India.

***Acharya** (in a serious tone):*

"Hmph... Do you really think she came back to India just to escape? Both she and that Englishman, Richard Robertson, knew very well what could happen if Jessica set foot in Hindustan."

(He said this while taking another sip of wine.)

***Osman** (in a frightened voice):*

"Sir, I mean no offense, but may I ask why you've had me searching for her all these years? ... For so long, I've done everything you've asked without question, but now, Sir, I... I want to know what this is all about and why we're chasing after her."

***Acharya** (while drinking):*

"To prevent a great catastrophe."

As soon as VIJAY touched that Yakshini locket, on one hand, Jessica started having seizures, on the other hand, Acharya started having seizures in the same manner in his bungalow in far away Delhi, just like Jessica had.

As soon as Vijay touched that gold locket, the tremors of the earthquake started being felt in the entire city of Sayal, Acharya's condition also started deteriorating in Delhi, 1000 kilometers away from Sayal, Acharya's eyes also started turning white and here Sayal Jessica's body started swinging 30 feet high in the air at a roadside dhaba just a few kilometers away from

Here in the Yakshini temple, as soon as Vijay pulled out the locket from the neck of the Yakshini idol, Jessica, who was swinging 30 feet in the air under someone's influence, suddenly falls on the ground, and here As soon as he pulled the golden gourd from the neck of the Vijay Yakshini idol in the temple, he felt the presence of someone in the temple, as if a wolf was in the temple.

A two-headed wolf comes out of the tunnels of the temple and moves towards Vijay growling with his red scary eyes, then to save his life he starts running away in fear of the falling wolf, the wolf pounces very fast towards Vijay but somehow while running, Vijay saved himself, despite Vijay's best efforts, the wolf injured Vijay by biting his hands, blood was flowing like water from Vijay's hand as the wolf was about to make its last attack towards Vijay. He moved forward, then Vijay moved his hands forward and suddenly the two-headed wolf suddenly stopped, stopped because Vijay had a gold locket in his hands, Vijay did not understand the wolf stopping like this. Where till a moment ago there was fear in his eyes, now there was fear in his eyes, the shining gold glow of the Yakshini idol was scaring the two headed wolf and within no time the wolf ran away in fear.

The wolf got scared and went back from where he came.

But Vijay thought of running away from there, he quickly gathered whatever he had in his hands, the soil of the Yakshini temple and the golden gourd, he filled all this in his bag and while running away, he was looking for a way out when he He moved towards the pond of the temple and then he fell into a tunnel like pit inside. Vijay was moving through that tunnel and was being swept by the flow of water and then Vijay reached the same place from where he had gone to that secret temple of Yakshini.

Here Jessica was very upset due to this strange supernatural incident that happened to her. Viren took hold of Jessica and said

Viren (worried):

"Jessica Ma'am, staying here is no longer safe for us in any way. We need to get out of here immediately."

Jessica was breathing hard, Viren somehow managed to take her along with him in the car and immediately left the place, there was a lot of chaos among the people around, for the first time in his life he felt something terrible like this, bad weather. And on top of that, the earthquake actually did not even have the feeling of victory as to what disaster it had unknowingly liberated by getting trapped in the whirlpool of its greed.

102 year old Robert Richardson living in London, Delhi based industrialist Acharya and NRI Jessica are all tied to the thread of Yakshini.

Jessica was completely unaware of her identity and Vijay of his future.

Vijay drives through the darkened village with the soil, returning to his workshop. The power cut casts shadows, but he places the soil bag inside.

Somehow, Vijay, while falling, returned to his home, saving his life. Saving his life from that forest, Vijay had recently returned to his home, saving himself from this unique magical experience that happened to him, but there too, Vijay had to wait for a minute. There was no peace because at that time it was 1 o'clock in the night and Vijay's wife Sujata had been waiting for her husband Vijay for the last several hours. While waiting for so long, even Sujata's worry had turned into anger. As soon as Vijay came home, When he reached the house, he closed the door and entered the house only to find his wife in front.

After Saying this Sujata went back to her room.There was lightning outside and Vijay was standing silently inside the house, completely broken due to his financial constraints and the tension going on at home, surrounded by clouds of anger and sadness, VIJAY goes to his workshop

The workshop where he He used to make idols but now his work has come to a standstill. Vijay had forgotten that magical experience he had a while ago due to a recent fight with his wife.

To forget his sorrow, VIJAY started drinking alcohol one after another. Started pegging, Vijay was drinking liquor one after the other non-stop, there was lightning outside.

Vijay said while talking to himself

Vijay (drunk):

"My entire life, I've been kicked around for this woman... And now, she's calling me stingy, huh. When I had money, she used to say I was the best husband in the world, and now... she curses everything, fights with me. That wretch accuses me of running around and spits in my face. If I had known earlier what a vile woman she is, I would've stayed a bachelor for life, but never married. And this Yakshini temple's soil is absolutely useless. Listening to that fool Rajan, I must've lost my mind. Took such a big risk for this Yakshini's soil... huh... useless."

Before VIJAY could say anything else, the lights in VIJAY's workshop went out due to the lightning outside. Vijay was drunk and in that condition he tries to stand. Vijay even stumbles here and there to find the torch. While trying to do so, his pair collides with something due to which his leg gets hurt and while muttering in anger, he shouts and says,

Vijay (angry):

"Damn it, today's been a complete disaster... Got all these injuries after wandering through that jungle, and now I have to come home and listen to this woman's nonsense."

Then Vijay's eyes fall on the sack.

Vijay:

"I faced the whole world... I went into that jungle... And damn it, I brought this... this useless dirt, you wretch!"

Saying this, Vijay started slamming the sack of Yakshini soil with great force. In his anger, fueled by rage and intoxication, Vijay had completely lost his mind.

Vijay:

"Six months without work, my wife cursing me day and night, no income, and on top of that, I even bought into these worthless superstitions."

Vijay sat down on his knees near the soil and said,

Vijay:

"Hey dirt... My friend Rajan says you made him rich overnight? You gave him a car, a house, money, and everything. So, why don't you do something for me too, sweetheart? Here, I'll even fold my hands... Make me immortal, make me rich, give me a millionaire's fortune... Come on, speak."

Saying this, Vijay calmed down a bit... He cursed his fate, then slumped against the wall, tears streaming down his face... He was muttering nonsense in his drunken state when suddenly, the lightning flashing outside startled him. Vijay saw the shadow of a terrifying woman's figure through the skylight of his workshop. Seeing this, Vijay, already frightened by the lightning, said,

Vijay (drunken):

"Did I drink a bit too much today?"

The sound of lightning stopped outside, and everything fell silent as the storm outside had completely subsided. Then, suddenly, there was a knock on the door of his workshop. Vijay was immediately gripped by fear because it was 3 o'clock in the morning—who could be at his door at this hour? Someone was knocking on the door of his workshop. Vijay sat there, listening to the knocking from outside, wondering who it could be. Gathering all his courage, he called out,

Vijay:

"Who's there?... I said, who is it?"

The knocking stopped, but Vijay somehow managed to get on his feet and found a lantern nearby so he could see in the darkness who was knocking on his workshop door. With the lantern in hand, Vijay, with all the courage he could muster, opened the door of the workshop, only to find no one outside. Vijay, turning the lantern to the right, muttered to himself,

Vijay *(to himself):*

"Who the hell would come here at this hour...?"

Vijay was saying this while turning the lantern towards the left, when suddenly he saw a woman right in front of him and seeing this, Vijay got scared and hit the door of his workshop, due to which he slipped behind, that mysterious looking woman. She was very beautiful in appearance, thick and long black hair from head to waist, a very beautiful red colored saree,

beautiful fair body, red lips, the entire body was laden with gold ornaments from top to bottom, a waistband around the waist. It felt as if a woman had come directly from ancient times or heaven to this human earth. There was darkness all around and in that dark isolated environment, where did a very beautiful but mysterious woman come from? Vijay was getting worried thinking this.

The flickering light of a lantern casts a dim glow, revealing the modest surroundings of Vijay's dwelling. The room is filled with a hushed stillness, broken only by the soft crackle of the lantern's flame.

VIJAY was peeping outside his workshop in the light of the lantern, Vijay took a look at both his right and left sides, first not finding anything in that direction, as he turned the lantern in the other direction, then suddenly suddenly A woman with a very scary face was seen in front of her. The stormy weather and the harsh cold made Vijay feel badly, her face started looking even more scary in the light of the lightning in the terrible stormy night.

Due to which the lantern fell from Vijay's hands to the ground and Vijay screamed in fear, but as soon as Vijay opened his eyes, he saw the figure of a woman in front of him in the darkness, Vijay was picking up the torch in his hands. Turning the yellow light of the lantern towards that woman, Vijay saw a very beautiful woman standing in front of him in a red sleeveless saree, with long thick hair, thin waist and a gold waistband on her waist, several gold rings on her fingers. Saree, rings, big gold jewelry around the neck, means the whole body is laden with gold, fair body, beautiful shoulders, big attractive breasts, light curly hair, as if she was an angel from heaven because as soon as she arrived, a wonderful fragrance spread all around. ,

And the most surprising thing was that the face of that unknown and beautiful woman was exactly similar to Jessica.

Where Vijay was till now scared of the shadow of that woman, now the same woman was standing in front of Vijay in a very attractive and mesmerizing form, Vijay controlled himself and said

Vijay:

"Madam, who are you....?"

Vijay said while looking around.

Vijay:

"And what are you doing here at this hour?"

Saying this, Vijay looked at the woman's attractive body from top to bottom. Seeing her, Vijay lost his consciousness for two minutes. Then the unknown woman spoke, which diverted Vijay's attention from her.

Unknown Woman (in a mesmerizing voice):

"Are you going to keep staring at me like this, or... invite me inside?"

Vijay thought to himself.

Vijay (thinking):

"First, this stormy night... and now this woman, how did she end up here? Her whole body is adorned with gold jewelry."

Unknown Woman:

"What's the matter, Vijay? Will you keep talking to yourself, or will you invite me inside?"

Vijay:

"Yes... No, no... Just a minute, madam. What could you possibly need from me at this late hour? On top of this storm, you show up in the dark, covered in jewelry. You have no idea how risky this could be for you."

Unknown Woman (pointing a finger):

"Sssshhh..."

Saying this, the unknown woman entered the workshop, walking as if she were a queen or princess. Vijay followed her inside and saw that she was examining each idol in his workshop, the same idols whose orders had been canceled due to the lockdown.

Vijay rushed inside and said:

Vijay (frightened):

"Madam, please leave right now. I'm not alone here; my wife and son are with me. If they see you here at this hour, it will cause unnecessary trouble... so you need to leave immediately."

The unknown woman stopped Vijay again and said:

Unknown Woman:

"Vijay, if I leave now, you and your wife will also be gone by tomorrow morning... Whatever remains with you will be lost."

Vijay (shocked):

"How do you know my name? And all this... How do you know so much about me? Who are you?"

Suddenly, lightning struck again, and the woman replied:

Unknown Woman:

"Who am I? Where do I come from? Why am I here? My one answer will erase all the troubles you've been enduring for the past year."

Vijay:

"What do you mean?"

Unknown Woman:

"I've heard that you are a very skilled sculptor... I have a task for you. You need to create a statue that looks exactly like me, just like me."

Vijay (irritated):

"It's so late, madam. Please, don't joke with me. I've worked day and night to make these statues, and I haven't earned a single penny. People order statues but create a drama when it comes to payment, and now, with the lockdown, who will buy these?"

Then the woman took out a large, beautiful, and shiny gold ring from her hand and extended it towards Vijay. The shine of the ring dazzled Vijay, and all his irritation and anger evaporated. He said:

Vijay:

"But, madam..."

Before he could say anything further, the woman replied:

Unknown Woman:

"Whatever you do for me, you will receive its value immediately."

Vijay:

"But... What exactly do I need to do?"

Unknown Woman:

"You must create a statue for me that is exactly like me, a perfect replica. I will come to you only three times. Each time I visit, I will check the progress of the statue you are making of me. Only then will you receive your payment in full."

Vijay thought in his mind

Vijay (thinking to himself):

"This seems right... If someone is offering me work, why should I refuse? It's beneficial for me."

The unknown woman took out her very precious gold ring and offered it to Vijay. Hesitatingly, Vijay showed some *confusion on his face and said:*

Vijay:

"Madam, I don't take jewelry. If you must give something, please..."

Unknown Woman:

"This is all I have for now... and for your future work, you'll be compensated with gold as well."

Vijay thought to himself:

Vijay *(thinking):*

"First, I have no work or money, and this woman is offering so much money for such a small task. One should never refuse a blessing that comes their way. She has no idea of the value of this ring. Yes, just say yes... just say yes."

Then the unknown woman said:

Unknown Woman:

"Don't overthink it... Take the ring for your work, but remember, if anyone learns about our deal, you will lose everything you've gained."

Saying this, she held the ring towards Vijay. As soon as Vijay extended his hand to take the ring and touched it, he felt a strange prick in his hand. A small drop of blood came out from Vijay's finger and fell onto the woman's other hand. Vijay's blood mingled with the woman's hand. There was a terrible thunderstorm outside, and a strange glow appeared in the woman's eyes as she said:

Unknown Woman:

"Now you belong to me... until your last breath."

Once again, there was a thunderous crash, so terrifying that even Vijay was frightened for a moment. In the lightning's light, the woman's face looked very frightening, causing Vijay to scream.

Screen fades to black.

Next Morning:

Viren and Jessica were at a hospital in Sayal City. The strange incidents from the previous night had shaken Jessica so much that she had been unconscious since then. Viren stayed beside her to care for her.

Jessica slowly regained consciousness, and as soon as she did, Viren said:

Viren:

"Ma'am, please, just rest..."

Jessica:

"What exactly happened to me last night?"

Viren:

"Ma'am, it might be better if you don't ask. Last night, you had strange seizures. Thankfully, everything stopped in time."

Jessica:

"Viren, please, tell me exactly what happened."

Viren hesitated, afraid of how the strange incident might affect Jessica's mind.

Jessica (angry):

"Viren... I'm asking you! Tell me what happened last night!"

Seeing Jessica's frustration, Viren finally spoke:

Viren:

"Ma'am... When your seizures started, at first, only your body was shaking. But then, your eyes turned completely white. It was so frightening that even I was scared. After that, you seemed to return to normal, but soon the seizures started again and then..."

Jessica:

"What happened after that?"

Viren:

"Ma'am, during the second seizure, your entire body began to levitate in the air. Your eyes turned white again, and the atmosphere around us became eerily frightening."

Jessica was surprised to hear all this and said

Jessica (being upset)

Oh My God...............

That means my grandfather was right!

This curse and all this is true

We have to find that temple of Yakshini as soon as possible, otherwise who knows what else can happen in the future. ,

Viren and Jessica are about to leave the hospital immediately after clearing their pending bills, Jessica was covering her face with a scarf so that no one would recognize her, but in the same hospital itself, a man's eyes fall on them, it is the same person. There was a man who had eaten last night at the same dhaba where Viren and Jessica had had tea the previous night and he had seen Jessica having a seizure, that man was a resident of Sayal city, his name was Dinesh, Dinesh secretly Chased them both, while Jessica and Viren immediately sat in their car and left from there.

Standing at the door of the hospital, Dinesh immediately took out his mobile from his pocket and Took a picture of Viren's car

Vijay was sleeping very deeply at his home, suddenly Viren started seeing terrible scenes of the previous night in his dreams, then suddenly Viren's eyes opened and he found himself at his home. Lying in the outer room of the house i.e. the drawing room, Vijay took a sigh of relief and while talking to himself, cleaning his eyes and mouth, said

Vijay (breathing a sigh of relief):

"So it was all just a dream... Good God, what happened last night was no less than a nightmare."

Vijay:

"But wait...! The fight with Sujata was real, right? Oh no..."

Shocked by the memory of his argument with his wife, Vijay rushed to his room. Finding Sujata and their son Shubham sleeping soundly, Vijay breathed a sigh of relief. Slowly walking back to the drawing room, he muttered:

Vijay:

"Thank God... They're still here. But what about the money? How will I arrange it?"

Suddenly, Vijay felt a strange prick in his hands. He looked at his hand and realized it was from the ring given to him by the unknown woman last night. His head began to spin as he recalled everything from the previous night. He reached into his pocket and found the ring—his advance payment for the work.

Vijay:

"So everything that happened last night was real... It was all true. I need to go tell Sujata. She'll be so happy!"

Vijay was excited and was about to tell this to his wife, when suddenly the words of that unknown woman started ringing in his ears, he remembered that that woman had told Vijay not to tell anything to anyone, Vijay said while talking to myself

***Vijay** (talking to himself):*

"Not only did I finally get a job after so much struggle, but now I'm stuck with this fool. If I tell this idiot everything, he either won't understand or will think I'm having an affair with the woman who gave me this job. But who was that woman anyway? She didn't even tell me her name."

Looking at the precious ring in his hands, Vijay said:

***Vijay** (while looking at the ring):*

"Well, you're the one who'll fix my poverty now."

Cut to:

Vijay had called his jeweler friend, Dinesh, to make a deal for the ring. Dinesh was the same person who had been watching Jessica and Viren from the hospital and had taken pictures of their car. He was also present at the dhaba last night. Now, Dinesh had come to deal with the precious ring.

Dinesh:

"Brother, where were you last night? You have no idea what weird things I saw."
Vijay:
"Forget about it. What I went through last night... nothing compares."
Dinesh:
"What are you talking about? The storm last night was..."
Vijay cut him off:
Vijay:
"Enough, enough... There's no point discussing this now. Let's focus on the reason I called you. Did you bring the money?"
Dinesh:
"Yes, I have the money. But why are you selling your wife's jewelry? If you need help, I can give you money. Just return it whenever you can. I'm not saying you need to sell the jewelry right now."
Vijay realized that Dinesh thought he was selling Sujata's jewelry due to financial problems. Vijay thought to himself:
Vijay (talking to himself):
"It seems he doesn't know this ring belongs to someone else. It's better this way; he won't question me about it. Otherwise, he'd drive me crazy asking about the ring."
Lost in his thoughts, Vijay didn't notice when Dinesh gently placed his hands on Vijay's shoulders.
Dinesh:
"Are you listening, Vijju?"
Vijay was slightly shocked when this happened
Vijay:
"Yes... Sorry, I've been a bit disturbed since last night."
Saying this, Vijay took out a box of rings from his pocket and showed it to Dinesh.
Vijay:

"Now tell me... How much can I get for this? It's an old ring! Belonged to Sujata's grandfather."

In his mind, Vijay thought the ring would be worth 2-3 lakhs, but he intended to exaggerate its value to get more money from Dinesh.

Dinesh slowly took the ring from Vijay's hands. The ring had such a mesmerizing shine that anyone who looked at it would be drawn to it. Dinesh stared at the ring, his eyes dazzled by its brilliance.

Vijay:

"Now tell me how much I'll get for it..."

Dinesh:

"Are you sure this is Sujata Bhabi's?"

Vijay:

"Of course. It's a family heirloom. Sujata brought it from her family."

Dinesh:

"Do you have the papers for it?"

Vijay:

"Come on... It's a family heirloom passed down through generations. Who kept papers for such old jewelry? Where would I get those papers from?"

In his mind, Vijay thought:

Vijay (talking to himself):

"This fool has no idea where this ring came from. It's worth 2-3 lakhs; I just need to get double the amount."

Dinesh:

"But without papers..."

Vijay (irritated):

"Dinesh, if you can't give me the money for this ring, just tell me now. I'll go somewhere else. Don't bother asking for papers now. Just give me the money."

Seeing Vijay's irritation, Dinesh was completely captivated by the ring. To calm Vijay down, Dinesh responded:

***Dinesh** (calming Vijay):*

"Hey, Vijay, why are you getting so angry over small things? I never said I wouldn't buy the ring. Look, this ring could be worth around 14 lakhs, but since you don't have the papers and you need money urgently, I can offer you half, which is 7 lakhs. Is that okay with you?"

Hearing this, Vijay was overjoyed. In his mind, he thought:

***Vijay** (spoken to himself):*

"This idiot has fallen for it..."

Dinesh then took out a bundle of money from his bag and handed it to Vijay.

Dinesh:

"Here you go, Vijay... It's a full 7 lakhs. Since this is an unofficial deal, I can't provide a full receipt."

***Vijay** (taking the money):*

"This much money is enough for me. At least I won't need to borrow from anyone now."

***Dinesh** (putting the ring in his bag):*

"Vijay Bhai, if you have any good deals in the future, make sure to remember us."

***Vijay** (happy):*

"Absolutely, Bhai... You have no idea how much you've helped me during this recession. By the way, you mentioned something about seeing something strange last night. Was there any crime or something?"

As Dinesh drove away, he couldn't help but smile to himself, marveling at his good fortune. The ring's true value was far beyond what Vijay had imagined, and Dinesh felt a sense of satisfaction in both his financial gain and the clever manipulation involved.

***Dinesh** (to himself, with a smirk):*

"Looks like Vijay's ignorance has worked in my favor. This ring will fetch me a fortune, and he'll never know what he let go."

He continued driving, his thoughts racing with plans for the ring. The excitement of his lucrative find was evident in his every word and expression.

Cut to -

Omar (entering his office, shocked):

"What the—? What is this?"

On Omar's desktop screen, there was an urgent alert showing a series of strange and alarming images related to the ring. Among the images was a detailed diagram indicating a network of people involved with occult practices. There were also photos of the ring and its connections to a series of mysterious events and dark rituals.

Omar (to himself):

"These... these images... they're showing a connection between the ring and some sinister activities. This can't be a coincidence."

He quickly picked up his phone and dialed Acharya.

Omar (urgently):

"Sir, you need to see this. The alert on my computer is showing something incredibly disturbing. It's about the ring and some dark practices."

Acharya (worried, coughing):

"Show me everything you can. This is more important than I realized."

As Omar shared the screen with Acharya, Acharya's expression grew graver.

Acharya:

"This ring is not just a cursed artifact. It's a key to something far darker. This confirms my fears—something terrible is about to unfold. We need to act fast."

Omar:

"Sir, what should we do? How do we stop this?"

Acharya:

"First, we need to find out who else is involved and understand their motives. The ring has been passed around, and now it's in the hands of someone who might be using it for evil purposes. We must track down Dinesh and uncover everything about this ring and its history."

Omar:

"I'll start by reaching out to Dinesh and try to get more information. But we should also inform others who might be in danger."

Acharya:

"Yes, and we need to be cautious. The influence of the ring can reach far and wide. Everyone involved is at risk."

As Omar set out to contact Dinesh and investigate further, Acharya remained in deep thought, knowing that the ring's dark legacy was far from over. The revelation marked the beginning of a new and perilous chapter that would test their resolve and understanding of the supernatural forces at play.

CUT TO

IN THE Town of Sayal

What actually happened was that someone had secretly made a video of the sudden seizure that Jessica had suffered at the roadside dhaba last night, due to which Jessica started swinging 15 feet in the air, and what's more, that person had also posted this The video was also posted on social media and made viral, there was no one else and only one person who could do this and that was Dinesh Sayal, a jeweler from the city, Dinesh, so Dinesh was trying to show that video to his friend Vijay.

Here in the hotel lodge, Viren and Jessica are watching the same clip of last night on the TV of their hotel lodge as TV news, this clip was going viral everywhere, from people's mobile phones to WhatsApp and Instagram everywhere.

Out of fear, Jessica covered her face with a cloth and Viren also covered her face with a hat and cap and went to the hotel room.

Sujata (confused):

"But Vijay, it's not just about the money. Where did all this sudden wealth come from?"

Vijay (irritated):

"Yaar, just focus on handling the money and stop asking so many questions. I told you, I got a new job, and that's where the money came from."

Sujata (still concerned):

"New job? But in this recession? And why are you so tense? I'm just worried."

Vijay (raising his voice):

"Enough! Just stop with the questions. You're making me crazy with all this probing. The money's here, and that's all that matters. If you have any more complaints, just keep them to yourself."

Sujata (sighing):

"Alright, Vijay. I hope you know what you're doing."

Vijay (muttering to himself):

"Better keep her quiet. The last thing I need is more trouble."

As Vijay and Sujata's conversation ended, Vijay's new car sat gleaming outside, a symbol of his sudden financial windfall. Vijay, still basking in his recent success, was determined to enjoy the fruits of his new-found wealth, even if it meant dealing with Sujata's concerns.

Meanwhile, in Agartala, Professor Anuj Baruah was deep in thought. He had just received more information about the mysterious video involving Jessica.

Anuj (to himself, serious):

"If this footage is real, then the girl is in grave danger. The legends about this Yakshini are no joke. I must find out more and warn whoever is in peril."

The air was thick with tension as Jessica, Viren, and Anuj gathered around the old wooden table in the dusty archives of the museum. The trio had come together for a singular purpose: to unravel the mystery surrounding the enigmatic sculptor, Mohit, whose untimely death had left a lingering cloud of fear and intrigue.

Jessica brushed her fingers over the cover of a worn diary, its leather bound frayed at the edges. "This is it. This is Mohit's diary," she said, her voice a mixture of excitement and trepidation. Viren leaned closer, intrigued, while Anuj adjusted his glasses, his scholarly demeanor ready to absorb every detail.

"Let's see what he has to say," Viren urged, and with a nod from Jessica, she opened the diary, the pages cracking slightly as they parted.

As they began to read, Jessica's voice echoed in the small room. *"I never believed in the supernatural, but sometimes, life forces you to question your beliefs."*

Mohit's writing flowed in a tortured manner, reflecting the turmoil of his life. He recounted the struggles of being a sculptor in a world ravaged by the pandemic. The lockdown had crippled his business, leaving him in debt and desperate. *"I was corrupt. My art, once a passion, became a commodity to survive. The days blurred into one another, filled with anxiety and the haunting sounds of the empty streets."*

Jessica glanced up, exchanging worried looks with Viren and Anuj. "He seems to be at the end of his rope," she whispered.

Continuing, Jessica read about a day when Mohit's son returned home with a strange bag of soil he had found in the nearby reserved forest. *"He said it was magical, that it held the essence of the earth. I laughed it off, dismissing it as childish fantasy."*

Anuj's brow furrowed. "The reserved forest? Legends say that it's a place of old spirits. Perhaps that soil had more significance than he realized."

Jessica nodded, focusing on the next entry. *"As I worked with the soil, I felt an energy unlike anything I had ever experienced. My hands became nimble, my creativity flowing as if guided by an unseen force."*

Days turned into weeks, and Mohit described a fateful rainy night that would change everything. *"I was in my workshop, lost in the rhythm of sculpting, when she appeared. A beautiful woman, her skin glistening like the rain, approached me."*

Viren leaned forward, intrigued. "A classic horror setup. What did she want?"

Jessica continued reading, her heart racing. *"She asked me to create an idol of a woman like her and handed me a golden necklace as payment. I was entranced by her beauty, and I accepted without hesitation."*

As the entries progressed, Mohit's demeanor shifted. *"I became obsessed with the idol. It was as if she had a hold on me. I could hear whispers in the night, urging me to carve deeper, to capture her essence. I didn't realize I was losing myself."*

Viren exchanged glances with Anuj, who was now scribbling notes furiously. "This is remarkable," he muttered, clearly captivated by the tale.

Jessica's voice trembled as she read further. *"One night, I dreamed of her. She was angry, accusing me of misrepresenting her beauty. When I woke, I found the idol had transformed, its features grotesque, almost mocking me."*

Anuj leaned back, a chill running down his spine. "What happened next?" he asked, his curiosity piqued.

"I thought I could control it, but the idol became my master. I was cursed, and I had no way to escape. My son pleaded with me to stop, but I couldn't. The whispers became screams."

Jessica's voice dropped to a whisper, her eyes wide. "He thought he was being possessed."

Anuj rubbed his chin thoughtfully. "This is where the legend might be rooted. The idea of art consuming the artist. It's tragic."

In the next entry, Mohit described a night when everything changed. *"I was in my workshop, the storm raging outside. The idol glowed with a malevolent light, and I could feel the presence of the woman within it, her anger seeping into my soul. I couldn't escape."*

Viren leaned back, panic rising in his chest. "What happened next?"

"I struck the idol in a fit of rage, and that's when I saw her face. Not beautiful, but twisted in agony. I had trapped her spirit within my creation. I realized too late the consequences of my actions."

As they neared the end of the diary, Jessica's voice quivered with emotion. *"I cannot escape this curse. I have locked away a part of her within the idol, and now it demands a price. I fear for my son. If anyone should be harmed, it will be him."*

Jessica looked up, her eyes shimmering with unshed tears. "He was terrified for his son," she murmured.

"If you find this diary, please heed my warning. Do not let greed blind you. The artist must respect the spirit of the art, or suffer the consequences."

Dr. Sharma closed the diary gently. "What a tragic tale. He lost everything because he ignored the warnings of the universe."

As the three sat in silence, absorbing Mohit's story, the air around them grew heavy with foreboding. Jessica felt a shiver run down her spine. "I can't shake the feeling that this isn't just a story. It feels real, like he's warning us from beyond the grave," she said softly.

Viren nodded. "We should find the idol. Maybe it's still in his workshop. There could be answers there."

Anuj shook his head, looking pensive. "Be cautious. If the legend holds any truth, we might be dealing with forces beyond our understanding."

Determined to uncover the truth, the trio made their way to Mohit's abandoned workshop, located at the edge of the reserved forest. The sun began to set, casting long shadows as they approached the crumbling building.

Jessica felt a sense of dread as they entered, the smell of damp earth and decaying wood engulfing them. Viren flicked on his flashlight, illuminating the chaotic remnants of Mohit's once-thriving studio. Sculptures lay scattered, some half-finished, others broken and forgotten.

"Where do we even start?" Jessica asked, her heart pounding.

Anuj moved cautiously toward a corner, his eyes catching something glinting. "Over here! I think I found it."

As they gathered around the pedestal, the sight of the idol sent chills down their spines. It was a hauntingly beautiful representation of a woman, yet something about it felt off. The features were too perfect, too alive.

"Look at its eyes," Viren whispered, stepping back slightly. "It feels like it's watching us."

Anuj reached out tentatively, his fingers grazing the idol's surface. "This is remarkable craftsmanship. But..." He hesitated, a frown crossing his face. "It feels wrong."

Jessica stepped closer, entranced. "I need to touch it," she said, her voice barely above a whisper.

"Jessica, wait!" Viren warned, but it was too late.

As Jessica's fingers made contact with the idol, a surge of energy coursed through her. The room darkened, and the whispers Mohit had described filled the air, growing louder and more frantic.

"Jessica!" Viren shouted, but she was lost in a trance, her eyes glazed over.

The idol glowed ominously, and for a moment, Jessica saw visions—flashes of Mohit's life, his despair, and the woman's fury. It was overwhelming, pulling her deeper into the idol's curse.

Dr. Sharma tried to pull Jessica away, but an unseen force held her fast. "Let her go!" Viren yelled, panic rising in his chest. He grabbed a nearby sculpture and hurled it at the idol, shattering it into pieces.

The idol cracked, and a deafening scream erupted from it, shaking the very foundation of the workshop. Jessica fell to her knees, gasping for air as the energy dissipated.

When the chaos finally subsided, the room fell silent. Jessica looked around, disoriented, while Viren rushed to her side.

"What just happened?" she asked, her voice trembling.

Anuj knelt beside the broken idol, studying the shards. "We broke the curse, but at what cost?" he murmured.

As they left the workshop, the weight of Mohit's story lingered in the air. The sun dipped below the horizon, casting eerie shadows in their wake.

Jessica glanced back at the now-destroyed idol, feeling a strange sense of loss. "We should honor his memory, find a way to remember him without the curse," she said.

Anuj nodded, his heart heavy. "We owe him that much."

But as they turned to leave, a sudden chill swept through the air, sending shivers down their spines. The ground beneath them trembled, and dark clouds rolled in from the distance, blocking out the fading sunlight.

"What's happening?" Viren asked, his voice rising with fear.

Anuj's face turned pale as he recalled the diary's warning. "This isn't over. Mohit's spirit is restless. We may have awakened something we can't control."

As they hurried away, a low rumble echoed from the forest. The whispers from the idol grew louder, calling to them, beckoning them back to the darkness.

In the days that followed, strange occurrences began to plague their lives. Shadows danced just beyond their

vision, and nightmares haunted their sleep. The curse of the Yakshini was far from broken, and they were now entangled in a web of darkness.

And as the sun set that night, they knew they had only scratched the surface of Mohit's tragic tale. The doomsday was just beginning, and they had unwittingly become part of a sinister legacy that threatened to consume them all.

The diary lay open on the table, its final pages fluttering in the wind as if whispering a warning. And somewhere deep within the forest, the spirit of the Yakshini waited, her curse poised to ensnare the next unsuspecting soul.

Anuj knew that the situation was becoming more complex and dangerous by the hour. The seemingly supernatural occurrences tied to the ring and the video were setting off alarms, and he had to act quickly to prevent any further catastrophe.

Back at Vijay's house, Sujata was left to contemplate the sudden turn of events. With Vijay's new car and the substantial amount of money, she couldn't shake the feeling that something was off. She decided to stay vigilant and keep an eye on her husband, hoping that whatever was happening would not lead to more problems.

As the night fell, the various threads of the story began to weave together, hinting at a larger, more sinister plot involving the cursed ring, supernatural forces, and individuals who were unwittingly caught in its web.

After scolding his wife like this, Vijay again walked out of the house in anger.

As soon as Dinesh reached his home, he showed that precious ring to his wife Renu, actually Renu is the same girl whom we saw in the beginning of the story, yes, the same girl who became a victim of Yakshini's deception after coming near J-J Colony Milestone 3km. Was ,

Renu is also an archaeologist by profession. As soon as Dinesh came home, he showed the precious ring to his wife and said

***Dinesh** (showing the ring to his wife Renu):*

"Before you ask where this ring came from or who gave it to me, let me tell you that this ring... I got it from Vijay. And that fool sold me this priceless antique piece for just 7 lakhs."

Renu's eyes widened in amazement as she looked at the ring.

***Renu**:*

"An antique ring sold for so little? Wow... But are you sure it's really antique?"

***Dinesh**:*

"I need confirmation from you. Since you're an archaeological expert, please take it to your lab and find out if it's truly antique and, if so, how old it is. Just let me know, please."

Renu, who was complicit in her husband's illicit activities, often helped him smuggle valuable artifacts and jewels. She agreed to check the ring's authenticity.

***Renu**:*

"Alright, give me until tonight. I'll do the carbon dating and get back to you."

Meanwhile, in Delhi, Acharya, who was struggling with his illness, was desperate to uncover the secrets of the ring sent by Dinesh. He knew that the ring could be extremely dangerous.

***Acharya** (breathing heavily):*

"You... you need to ask your friend where that ring came from... from where it came to him..."

Omar, concerned for his boss's health, was trying to comfort him and take care of his needs, but Acharya was adamant about finding out more about the ring. Despite the pain, Acharya removed his oxygen mask and continued speaking.

***Omar**:*

"Sir, please take care of yourself. We're trying to contact your friend, but he hasn't given us any other contact number. He only reaches out when necessary from a separate number... Please, just rest for now."

***Acharya** (breathing heavily):*

"No, Omar... I don't have time for that now. First, this girl... Jessica... and now this ring..."

***Omar**:*

"What's so special about this ring, sir?"

Acharya looked at the Yakshini painting, its eerie presence seeming to come alive in his troubled gaze.

***Acharya**:*

"This ring has erased the legacy of great empires. Its gold brings nothing but destruction... because this gold is cursed."

Omar, sensing the gravity of the situation, was already trying to trace Dinesh through his social media accounts. He received a notification on his tablet about a video Dinesh had posted on Instagram from the previous night. Omar showed the video to Acharya, who was instantly struck by shock and fear.

***Acharya** (eyes widening in surprise):*

"This... this is the ring... How did it end up with him?"

Omar, realizing the potential danger, continued watching the video with Acharya. The revelation that Dinesh had the ring added a new layer of urgency to their mission.

***Acharya**:*

"Whatever happens, we must retrieve that ring. It's not just an antique; it's a source of immense danger. We must act quickly."

Omar, understanding the gravity of the situation, prepared to act swiftly. The interconnectedness of the cursed ring, Dinesh's illicit dealings, and the emerging threats pointed towards a looming disaster that needed immediate intervention.

Cut to -

The video which Omer and Acharya had seen on their tablets and left the square, Jessica and Viren were also watching on their mobiles sitting in VK Lodge in Sayal, actually this video was from last night in which Jessica got possessed in a mysterious and horrifying manner. This was seen happening and was flying in the air and Dinesh had secretly made a video of it and posted it on his Instagram.And within no time this video went viral on Instagram, Jessica was watching this video when Viren came to her and said

Viren:

"Ma'am, it's not safe to stay here much longer. We need to act quickly because Acharya could arrive here at any moment."

Jessica:

"We need someone who can provide us with information about the Yakshini and her history, someone with extensive knowledge about the lost kingdom of Sayal."

Jessica said this while examining the precious gold bracelet she was holding.
Viren:
"There is someone who can help us with that!"
Viren and Jessica's urgency was palpable as they sought out the expert who could provide them with the critical information they needed.

Cut to -
The wealth of money in Vijay's house had doubled in two days and quadrupled in one night. Vijay had sold his old idle car and bought a new car a day ago, but today two electronic devices were found at his house simultaneously. Delivery was done, one AC and another LCD TV, Vijay's neighbors were quite surprised by his sudden progress and even more surprised was his wife Sujata, Sujata was watching all this from the door of the house and Vijay was driving at the tempo. He was getting both the goods unloaded

Within half an hour, the technicians got both the appliances properly fitted in the house and went away, but Vijay handed over 5 rupee notes from his pocket to those technicians as a gratuity. Seeing this, Sujata and It also felt strange and she wondered whether her husband was doing illegal work to Vijay? And with this concern, Sujata asked Vijay after the technicians came out.
Sujata:
"Vijay.......!"

Enjoying the breeze from the new AC, Vijay stood near it, relishing the cool air in the scorching heat. His wife, Sujata, asked him with curiosity.

Sujata:

"Vijay......"

Vijay:

"Yeah, what is it?"

Sujata (curious):

"Can I ask you something?"

Vijay:

"Is it about where all this money came from? How did you suddenly get so much money in this recession? Who gave it to you?"

Sujata:

"Yes, that's it."

Vijay:

"I got a new job with a big company, and they made an advance payment. I used that money to clear my old debts."

Sujata:

"But what event is happening now? And during this time, with the lockdown..."

Vijay (ignoring):

"I have a lot of work to do right now. We'll talk later."

Ignoring his wife, Vijay went to his workshop, leaving Sujata with a growing suspicion that her husband was involved in something shady.

Nightfall

In a tense atmosphere, Viren and Jessica drove through a deserted road, while Renu, Dinesh's wife, drove home, unaware of the imminent danger. Vijay worked on the statue's structure in his workshop, following the instructions of the mysterious woman, while Renu headed towards her impending doom.

Meanwhile, Jessica and Viren reached the office of Dr. Anuj Sharma, an archaeologist who had seen the viral video of Jessica at the dhaba.

Dr. Anuj Sharma's Office

Anuj, an archaeology expert and senior lecturer at SAIL College, was working late into the night. Viren and Jessica arrived at his office with minimal difficulty, as there were not many people around. Jessica, who had to cover her face due to her viral video, removed her cloth as they entered Anuj's cabin.

Anuj:

"Yes, how can I help you?"

Viren:

"Sir, we need your help."

Anuj (noticing Jessica):

"Jessica? What are you doing here?"

Jessica, showing the priceless gold locket stolen from Yakshini's temple, explained her purpose. She had come to return the locket to save her grandfather, Robertson, from the curse of immortality.

Anuj:

"I have a question. You are educated and born in London; do you really believe in these superstitions?"

Jessica:

"Like you, I didn't believe in them either. But after everything I've experienced recently, I've realized that sometimes human understanding is limited, and where our knowledge ends, paranormal entities may begin."

Anuj:

"The forces you are dealing with are beyond life and death; this is not just about 1-2 years but a history of 400 years."

As Anuj spoke, he started narrating the ancient story of the Sayal dynasty and the Yakshini temple.

Anuj (narrating):

"The tale we are about to unravel begins centuries ago, in the year 1724, a time when the Indian subcontinent was a landscape of warring kingdoms and ambitious conquerors. Among these ruthless figures was a formidable Afghan invader, whose name was whispered in fear and awe across the lands. His reputation was one of absolute dread—a warlord whose insatiable hunger for power was matched only by his brutal methods. His army was not merely a force but a relentless tide of destruction, sweeping away all in its path with terrifying efficiency.

This Afghan marauder was not content with the mere accumulation of wealth and territory. His ambitions soared far beyond the material, reaching for a prize of otherworldly significance. He sought a power so profound that it could make even death itself yield before him. This was no ordinary conquest; he was in pursuit of an ancient and mystical force rumored to be so formidable that it could render the most dazzling jewels and gold utterly insignificant by comparison.

The whispers of this immense power led him to the remote and enigmatic Sayal Kingdom, a small but fabled realm located in the northeastern fringes of India. Sayal was shrouded in an aura of legend and secrecy, said to be a land where magic and divine protection intertwined. The tales spoke of a force so great that it could compel even the gods to kneel. It was an irresistible lure for the marauder, whose unrelenting greed drove him to target this secluded kingdom.

Determined to seize this unparalleled power, the marauder dispatched his most trusted general with a colossal army of 500,000 soldiers—an assembly of the fiercest warriors, trained and conditioned for total war. This invasion force was a *veritable ocean of men, their sheer numbers intended to obliterate any resistance and secure their dominion over Sayal. The army marched with grim purpose, their advance marked by an ominous silence that foretold the impending storm.*

As they approached the borders of Sayal, the heavens seemed to take notice. A dark, malevolent aura began to envelop the sky, casting a pall over the land. The air grew heavy with an unsettling chill, and the once-clear skies were soon filled with roiling, tempestuous clouds. It was as if the very natural world was bracing itself for the catastrophe that was about to unfold.

Yet, what happened next defied all rational explanation. The Afghan army, an imposing and seemingly invincible force, began to dissolve into nothingness as soon as their boots touched the sacred soil of Sayal. Soldiers who had marched with such confidence and might were suddenly erased from existence, vanishing without a trace. The grandeur of their military campaign turned to a nightmarish enigma, their dreams of conquest evaporating into the ether.

The truth behind this cataclysmic event was rooted in the ancient and arcane powers that protected Sayal. For centuries, the kingdom had been shielded by a formidable enchantment, a spell of celestial origin that bound the very essence of the land. This was no ordinary curse but a complex weave of divine magic and primal forces, a pact forged by gods and ancient spirits to preserve the sanctity of Sayal's secrets.

The enchantment was a living entity, a sentient force that responded to threats with a vengeance that could only be described as divine retribution. The soil of Sayal itself was imbued with an otherworldly energy, a force that annihilated the invading army with an almost malevolent precision. The Afghan marauder's grand ambitions and his army's terrifying prowess were rendered powerless against this mystical shield.

The fate of the Afghan invaders became the stuff of dark legend, a cautionary tale of human hubris and the inscrutable forces that lie beyond mortal comprehension. The Sayal Kingdom remained an enigmatic beacon, its ancient power and protective curse preserving its hidden secrets from those who dared to seek them. The story of this invasion serves as a stark reminder of the limits of human ambition and the formidable, unfathomable forces that guard the mysteries of the ancient world. The secrets of Sayal, shrouded in layers of myth and magic, continue to elude those who would seek to uncover them, their tale forever etched into the annals of history as a testament to the unyielding might of a land that defied even the most fearsome of conquerors."

Renu's Situation

Meanwhile, Renu was trapped in JJ Colony's maze of illusions. Despite her efforts, she repeatedly encountered the same milestone, unable to find her way out.

Jessica (showing the gold locket):

"I need to return this to the Yakshini temple. It's the only way to save my grandfather."

Anuj:

"Until today, I only heard of such things in stories, but now I see them."

Jessica:

"What do you mean?"

Anuj:

"As I said before, this is not just about a few years; it's about a history of 400 years. The gold you are holding is actually a curse."

As the tension mounted, both Renu and Jessica faced their respective challenges, with the ancient curse and mysterious

powers intertwining their fates.
Viren:
"I have a question. What does all this have to do with Yakshini?"
Anuj:
"That's a story known to many, but have you ever wondered how the vast Afghan army disappeared overnight? Sayal was a very small state. How could it possibly stand against such a massive army?"

Meanwhile, Renu was driving back home, taking a shortcut from JJ Colony Road.
Renu (talking on the phone while driving):
"Sorry, sweetheart. I know you're upset, but I didn't realize how late it had gotten while wrapping up at the lab. Don't worry, I've finished the report and will email it to Sharma Sir tomorrow morning."
Dinesh (her husband, on the other side of the phone):
"It's okay. By the way, did you check the ring? Is it really antique?"
Renu (still on the phone):
"Yes, just one more day and I'll confirm it."
Dinesh:
"Just make sure it's an antique. I'm eager to see how we can make a fortune from it."
Renu:
"Did you eat yet? I left some food in the kitchen. Good, good. I'll be home in about 15 minutes. Wait, where am I now?"
Renu glanced out the window and noticed the milestone of JJ Colony again.
Renu:
"There's a JJ Colony milestone coming up again. Anyway, I was saying, for your birthday in a couple of days, why don't we

go out somewhere? I know it's short notice, but..."

As Renu continued talking, she noticed that the 3 km milestone of JJ Colony appeared once more, which startled her. She thought it might be a mistake or a trick of her tired mind.

Renu (to herself):

"How did I pass the JJ Colony milestone again? Maybe it's just my imagination. I must be confused from talking on the phone."

She got back in the car and drove forward, but the same milestone appeared again. This repeated occurrence made her anxious.

Renu (nervous):

"Something is definitely wrong. How am I ending up at the same place again and again? I haven't taken any turns. Why is this happening?"

Fearful and bewildered, she stopped the car, got out, and looked around. The area was eerily silent and dark, with only the headlights of her car illuminating the surroundings. The silence and darkness heightened her anxiety.

Renu (to herself, distressed):

"What is happening to me? I passed this milestone already. Why does it keep reappearing?"

Suddenly, Renu sensed a presence to her left and heard a faint scream that terrified her. She fell to the ground, but when she looked around, there was no one there. Her phone rang, breaking the silence.

Renu (hesitant, answering the phone):

"Hello...hello? Something strange is happening. The JJ Colony milestone keeps reappearing, and I saw a figure that screamed at me. I don't know what's going on."

Dinesh (on the phone):

"Honey, calm down. What happened? Are you okay? Should I come over there? Where are you?"

Renu, overwhelmed by fear and confusion, struggled to explain the bizarre events and the terrifying experience she was going through.

The girl was telling all these things to her husband on the phone when suddenly she started hearing a loud whirring sound from somewhere and when she slowly turned her head with frightened eyes, she found that actually her phone was in the car. lying there. Seeing this, the girl got a shock and then she looked at her mobile again with trembling hands in fear and remembered that after talking to her husband on the phone, she had left her mobile on the seat of the car. She had put it down, out of fear the phone fell from the girl's hand to the ground and the girl moved away from the phone in panic. .... She understood that some kind of thing is happening with her and the person with whom she has been talking for so long is not her pet but someone else.

Due to fear, the girl became very nervous and

And running fast towards the left side of the road, she started running very fast towards the farm and barn, now she had come out of the light of the street light and came into the light of the moon, running fast with heavy breath. That girl in the fields was running very fast to save her life from that unknown force, when she saw something in front of her in the field, which stunned her, suddenly we got to see the scene of the moon. A tree in light and a dead body hanging on that tree, this scene had filled the atmosphere with a strange graveyard-like silence.

In the light of the moon, that dead body hanging from the tree was very clearly visible to that girl, the girl who was running away to save her life from that unknown invisible black power, had now perhaps once again come in front of her in a panic and Then the girl saw that the dead body hanging from the tree slowly started rotating from back to front on its *own. The girl was holding her breath and watching this horrific scene with her own eyes, in the light of the moon.*

That dead body was now visible and as the dead body turned completely towards the girl, she found that the dead body with disheveled hair and blood soaked body was none other than the same girl herself, the same girl who had been saving her life for so long. She was running in the fields, seeing her dead body in front of her, the girl suddenly screamed and as if she was running again in the other direction in fear, her foot hit a stone and she fell on the ground and she saw that She has again reached the same place from where she had run away i.e. near the car. But then she realized something and said

INT. ANUJ'S OFFICE

The dimly lit office is a sanctuary of historical mysteries. Anuj, amidst ancient artifacts, narrates with a gravity that transforms the room into a portal of the past.

ANUJ: (Voice rich with historical depth)

In 1724, a massive Afghan army, numbering one hundred thousand, advanced from Delhi towards Assam. King Vishveshwar Pratap Baruah of Sayal had neither the strength nor the means to confront this formidable force. The atmosphere in the kingdom grew heavy with fear.

As Anuj speaks, the air thickens with an almost tangible sense of foreboding. The Aghori's entrance shifts the mood, adding a layer of supernatural menace.

AGHORI: (Voice echoing with dark prophecy)

RAJAN... YOUR KINGDOM'S IMPENDING DISASTERS CAN BE AVOIDED, BUT ONLY IF YOU SEEK OUT THE DEVI WHO WAS EXILED FROM THE HEAVENS.

Anuj, intrigued by the Aghori's cryptic message, leans forward, his curiosity piqued.

RAJA VISHVESHWAR: (With intense interest)

Which Devi are you referring to?

AGHORI: *(Voice dripping with enigma)*

THE ONE WHO CAN SUMMON A HUGE ARMY OVERNIGHT, WHO CAN DEVOUR AN ENTIRE KINGDOM, WHO CAN FILL THE OCEANS WITH ENDLESS GOLD. SHE WAS BANISHED FROM HEAVEN, IGNORED BY ALL, BUT WHOEVER WORSHIPS HER CAN HAVE THE WORLD AT THEIR FEET... *Yakshini.*

Anuj's expression reveals a mix of awe and comprehension as the significance of Yakshini becomes clear.

RAJA VISHVESHWAR: *(Eagerly)*

And then what happened?

ANUJ: *(Voice resonant with historical weight)*

The King created a hidden temple for Yakshini within the caves of Sayal's waterfalls and began her worship, defying the sacred texts and divine rules. Within eleven days, as the Afghan army approached Sayal's borders, Yakshini granted the King's wish. Her monstrous army of demons annihilated the Afghan force in one day, eradicating an entire army of one hundred thousand.

The room falls silent as Anuj's tale settles over the listeners, the ancient drama casting a dark shadow.

EXT. JJ COLONY ROAD - NIGHT

Renu's panic is palpable as she roams near her car, caught in an inexplicable and terrifying loop.

RENU: *(Frantic and tearful)*

Nothing is right here... I think I'm trapped. It's been half an hour, and I am stuck in a loop.

Her husband, Dinesh, struggles to understand her plight.

DINESH: *(On the phone, confused and concerned)*

What are you saying? I don't understand anything. Baby, where are you? Tell me so I can come pick you up.

RENU: *(Voice quivering)*

When I took a shortcut near the reserve forest, I saw a JJ Colony milestone marked 3km. But that same milestone keeps appearing over and over again. I haven't turned or reversed, but it's the same milestone. Even more horrifying, I saw a woman with disheveled hair and a terrifying face, and then she just disappeared.

DINESH: (Worried and trying to calm her)

What are you talking about? Just stay in the car and lock it. I'll come over immediately. Don't go outside the car. Stay on the phone with me.

Renu hangs up, feeling a chilling presence behind her. She turns to see a horrifying woman in red, soaked in blood, with disheveled hair and glittering gold jewelry. The woman reaches out her hand menacingly.

YAKSHINI: (In a chilling voice)

Return what is mine...

Renu's terrified gaze shifts to her car where her bag is kept. The horrifying woman advances, gouging Renu's eyes with her hands. Renu's scream echoes through the desolate night.

INT. ANUJ'S OFFICE - LATER

Anuj, Jessica, and Viren are deeply engrossed in their discussion.

ANUJ: (Solemnly)

King Vishveshwar saved Sayal from the Afghan invasion, but the cost was yet to be paid. One morning, darkness engulfed Sayal. The sunlight did not reach the kingdom. Strangely, only the palace on the hill was surrounded by lightning and dark clouds, as if a dreadful storm was hovering only over that place.

JESSICA: (Intrigued)

Did King Vishveshwar ever mention that there were no survivors in the royal family?

ANUJ: (Gravely)

The secret died with him. And honestly, I don't believe that returning the cursed gold to the temple will solve anything.

Jessica holds up a gold locket with a serious expression.

JESSICA: (Determined)

There must be a way to end this curse.

Vijay is working on an idol in his dimly lit workshop. The atmosphere is eerie, with strong winds and sporadic lightning. The lights flicker and go out.

VIJAY: (Irritated)

"Yeh bijli wale bhi... hamesha galat waqt par light cut kar dete hain!"

He curses, takes a swig from a liquor bottle, and starts online shopping, his mood lightening.

VIJAY: (Drunk, sarcastically)

"Us aurat ne mujhe itna ameer bana diya... Apne nuksaan se mujhe fayda. Chalo, aur mehngi cheezein kharidta hoon."

His phone dies, and he gazes at the idol uneasily. A shadow of a three-headed wolf appears in the dark.

VIJAY: (Fearful)

"K-k-kya tha yeh?"

The wolf lunges at him. Vijay screams and wakes up, relieved it was just a nightmare.

VIJAY: (Relieved, wiping sweat)

"Nahi! Yeh mera vehem tha!"

A knock on the door reveals the same beautiful woman from his dream, her face still hidden by darkness.

WOMAN: (Smiling)

"You've done a remarkable job, Vijay."

She inspects the idol, praises Vijay, and presents him with a precious gold locket.

WOMAN:

"This locket is for you, Vijay."

As it rains outside, the atmosphere turns romantic. Lightning reveals the woman's horrifying face.

VIJAY: (Shocked)

"Nahi! Yeh mera vehem hai!"

The romantic allure dissipates. The woman leaves, leaving Vijay unaware of the impending peril.

FADE OUT.

FADE IN: TITLE: "Yakshini Ka Shraap"

The scene transitions to Vijay's living room where he watches the news, visibly troubled.

NEWS ANCHOR (ON TV):

"In Sayal city, the body of Renu, an expert from the archeology department, was found in her car this morning. The city is in a state of panic."

Sujata enters, noticing Vijay's distress.

SUJATA:

"Vijay, what's wrong? Why do you look so worried?"

Anuj: "Aur dusri baat, jo insaan use mandir banane ka kaam karega, uska janm usi dharti ki mitti se hona chahiye. Tumhara dhyaan uski purani jameen par gaya, jahan tumne ek naye mandir ki buniyad rakhi thi."

Vijay: (Desperately) "Toh mujhe kya karna hoga? Kaise main is shraap se bach sakta hoon?"

Anuj: (Determined) "Sabse pehle, tumhe uss murti ko todna hoga, jo tumne banayi hai. Aur uske baad, tumhe uss dharti ki mitti ko dhundh kar wapas wahan le jaana hoga, jahan se tumne usse liya tha. Tumhare paas abhi bhi samay hai, par tumhe tezi se kaam karna hoga."

Jessica: (Nodding) "Haan, hum tumhari madad karenge. Tumhe ek pooja karni hogi aur usmein purane shraapit sona ko shamil karna hoga, taaki Yakshini ki shakti kam ho sake."

Viren: (Resolutely) "Chalo, humare paas bahut kam samay hai. Humein jaldi se plan banana hoga aur Yakshini ke saath is jang ko khatam karna hoga."

Vijay: (Nervously) "Main taiyaar hoon. Jo bhi karna hoga, main karunga. Lekin mere paas koi aur rasta nahi hai."

Anuj: "Acha, pehle tum apni aur apne doston ki suraksha ki soch lo. Tumhara purna dhyaan bas ek cheez par hona chahiye: Yakshini ko rokna. Tumhare saamne ek zordar ladayi hai, lekin tumhe ismein jeetna hoga."

Jessica: (Firmly) "Haan, hum tumhare saath hain. Abhi se shuru karte hain aur is shraap ko khatam karte hain."

CUT TO:

EXT. OLD TEMPLE - NIGHT

Vijay, Jessica, and Viren arrive at an ancient temple ruins, where Vijay had originally found the cursed soil. The atmosphere is eerie and tense as they navigate through the ruins.

Vijay: (Looking around anxiously) "Yeh wahi jagah hai. Humne yahin par woh shraapit sona rakha tha."

Jessica: (Examining the surroundings) "Humare paas jitna samay hai, usse kam se kam karenge. Tumhare dwara banayi gayi murti ko todna hoga aur dharti ki mitti ko wapas rakhna hoga."

Viren: (Determined) "Agar Yakshini ko rokna hai, toh humein sab kuch sahi karna hoga."

As they prepare for the ritual, the night grows darker, and the sense of foreboding intensifies. The Yakshini's presence is felt as shadows seem to move on their own.

CUT TO:

INT. TEMPLE RUINS - LATER

Vijay, Jessica, and Viren are performing the ritual, chanting ancient verses and placing the cursed soil back into its original spot. The tension is palpable as they work quickly.

Vijay: (Struggling) "Yeh bahut mushkil ho raha hai... lagta hai Yakshini humare saamne aa rahi hai."

Jessica: (Encouragingly) "Tumhe himmat nahi harni chahiye, Vijay. Tumhara yeh aakhri kadam hai."

Suddenly, the Yakshini appears in a burst of dark energy, her eyes glowing fiercely.

Yakshini: (Furious) "Tumhe yeh sab kuch nahi karne doongi! Tumne meri purani dharti ko chhoda aur mujhe shraapit kiya!"

Vijay: (Gritting his teeth) "Tumhare saath is shraap ko khatam karna hi hoga! Yeh sab kuch tumhare shraap ki wajah se hi ho raha hai!"

In a fierce battle of wills and strength, the group fights against the Yakshini's dark powers. With every chant and every movement, the energy in the temple shifts.

CUT TO:

The first light of dawn breaks through, illuminating the ruins. The temple seems to regain its former tranquility. The Yakshini's presence has vanished, and the cursed soil has been properly restored.

Jessica: (Relieved) "Humne yeh kar diya! Yakshini ki shakti kam ho gayi hai."

Viren: (Panting) "Haan, lekin ab bhi chinta hai. Humein dekhna hoga ki Yakshini ka shraap puri tarah khatam hua hai ya nahi."

Vijay: (Exhausted but hopeful) "Maine apna sab kuch kar diya hai. Ab aage ki raah kuchh shanti aur suraksha ki ummeed hai."

FADE OUT:

The screen fades to black, signaling the end of a harrowing chapter in Vijay's life. As the darkness recedes, there is a glimmer of hope that the curse has finally been lifted, and a new beginning awaits.

Certainly! Here's the screenplay written in narrative prose with a British accent:

Omar, bloodied and weak, sat on a chair as Acharya stood before him, his anger palpable.

Acharya, his voice edged with fury, demanded, "If you were determined to assist your brother Imaad, why did you alert us about Jessica's arrival in India?"

Omar, his voice feeble, replied, "I did it so that Imaad would believe in Jessica, and with that trust, she could reach the Yakshini temple."

Girish, Acharya's son, was seething with rage and drew his gun.

Girish, his voice trembling with anger, said, "Father, he's spouting nonsense. Let's just shoot him now."

Acharya stopped him, his voice resolute. "No, he still has much more to reveal."

Omar, despite his injuries, managed a weak laugh. "You will never defeat us. We are the last descendants of the Afghans."

In his fury, Girish aimed his gun at Omar's head and fired, killing him instantly.

Vijay's phone rang, jolting him from his distraught state. He answered it with trembling hands, an unknown number flashing on the screen.

Vijay, his voice cracking, asked, "Hello?"

Doctor (O.S.), the gravity of the situation evident in his tone, responded, "Your wife Sujata has been in an accident and is currently in the ICU. Her condition is critical."

Vijay's heart sank as he broke down in tears. He rushed to the hospital with Anuj and Jessica in tow.

At the hospital, the doctor briefed Vijay, Anuj, and Jessica on Sujata's dire condition.

*Doctor**, with a stern expression, informed them, "Sujata's condition is extremely precarious. She needs immediate surgery."*

The news of Shubham's death in the same accident shattered Vijay.

Vijay, *his voice breaking, said, "Shubham... no..."*

Jessica, *offering solace, said, "Yakshini has begun to show her wrath."*

In the morgue, Vijay was struck by the sound of Yakshini's eerie laughter.

Yakshini (V.O.), *her voice echoing, declared, "This is your punishment for deceiving me and breaking our pact. If you wish to save your wife, follow my instructions and create my idol."*

Vijay stood, paralysed by fear and grief.

In the dim light of his office, Anuj sat at his desk, a serious expression etched on his face as he prepared to share a story that had captivated him for years. Jessica and Vijay, seated across from him, sensed the gravity of the moment. The usual chatter faded, replaced by an attentive silence.

"Have you ever wondered why there's no one who can stand against Yakshini?" Anuj asked, his tone serious. "It's as if she's a force of nature, unmatched and unstoppable. But there's a story—a tale of a warrior princess who once stood strong against all odds. Her name was Durgawati, and she was a legend in her own time."

Jessica leaned in, intrigued. "What happened to her?"

Anuj continued, his voice steady. "Princess Durgawati was born under divine circumstances, a blessing from the gods. Her parents devoted their lives to prayer, and their faith was rewarded with her miraculous birth. From an early age, she exhibited remarkable beauty and strength. Trained in the arts of war, she became a master of archery and swordsmanship, leading her people with both skill and courage.

"She earned the title 'Warrior Princess' for her unmatched prowess in battle. Durgawati fought bravely to defend her kingdom against invaders, inspiring her people with her determination and strength. But as powerful as she was, there was an air of mystery surrounding her. Despite her victories, she often seemed burdened by something unseen."

Vijay frowned. "So, what happened? How could someone so powerful just vanish?"

Anuj's gaze darkened as he recounted the pivotal moment. "One day, without warning, Durgawati disappeared. One moment she was leading her kingdom; the next, she was gone. There were no signs of struggle, no clues as to where she might have gone. Her closest advisors searched tirelessly, but all efforts were in vain.

"Rumors spread quickly. Some believed she had been taken by the gods as a reward for her bravery. Others whispered of a curse placed upon her, one that had finally come to claim her. But no one could uncover the truth. As the years passed, Durgawati transformed from a legendary warrior into a myth, her tale fading into obscurity."

Jessica's expression turned somber. "So, she's now just a story?"

Anuj nodded gravely. "Exactly. A story that echoes through the ages, a reminder of her strength and the mystery of her disappearance. Though her legacy lives on, it serves as a haunting reminder that even the most powerful can vanish without a trace. The truth of her fate remains an enigma, buried beneath layers of time, waiting for someone brave enough to uncover it."

The room fell silent, the weight of Durgawati's story lingering in the air. In that moment, Anuj's narration *transformed the office into a space filled with unresolved questions and a deep sense of respect for a warrior who had once embodied strength and courage, now lost to history.*

FIVE

DOOMS DAY

Meanwhile, both Jessica and Acharya were experiencing severe seizures, reminiscent of Jessica's previous ordeal. The hospital staff were alarmed by Jessica's worsening condition, and a ward boy recognised her.

***Ward Boy**, with a hint of fear, murmured, "Isn't this the girl from that viral video...?"*

As chaos erupted, Vijay, Anuj, and Jessica fled the hospital.

Back at Acharya's safe house, Omar's lifeless body lay before them. Acharya's seizures had subsided, and Girish anxiously sought answers.

Girish, worried and confused, asked, "Father, what's happening? Why haven't you explained anything about Jessica or Yakshini?"

Acharya, gasping and visibly frightened, replied, "Because we are the link that stands as a barrier between Yakshini and this world..."

He then revealed a startling truth.

Acharya continued, "Robertson's British granddaughter, Jessica, we did not kidnap her to kill her but to protect her from reaching Yakshini."

Girish, stunned, questioned, "Why...?"

The car raced through the rugged terrain towards Sayal Reserve Forest. The weather turned increasingly violent.

Vijay, focused on driving, asked, "Anuj, how far is the secret temple?"

Anuj, lost in thought, replied, "Just a bit further. We need to destroy the idol and the *cursed gold here."*

Jessica, *puzzled, asked, "Vijay, you mentioned that Yakshini's face resembles mine?"*

Vijay, *serious, confirmed, "Yes, Jessica. When I first saw you, I was frightened. That might explain your strange visions."*

Jessica, *realising the connection, added, "So everything is interlinked. My grandfather's stolen gold is here too."*

As the car continued through the forest, the weather grew harsher—strong winds, thunder, and a red sky.

Anuj, urgently, said, "This is the prophecy. When Yakshini's powers increase, the sky will turn red and acid rain will follow. We're running out of time."

Vijay, determined, replied, "I'm increasing the speed. We need to get there quickly."

They spotted a milestone indicating "Sayal Reserve Forest 1 Kilometer."

Jessica, confused, asked, "Another milestone?"

Vijay, frowning, pondered, "Is this an illusion?"

Anuj, realising, said, "Yes, Yakshini is trapping us again. We need to take another route."

Vijay, resolute, agreed, "Alright, we'll take another route."

They veered onto a different path, accelerating. Meanwhile, the residents of Sayal city were panicking as the sky turned red.

Police Announcement

(loudspeaker)

"Please stay indoors. The weather is deteriorating."

Elderly Resident

(worried)

"This is a sign of a major disaster. Something terrible is about to happen."

The car approached a waterfall in the forest when a flock of crows attacked, cracking the windshield.

Vijay, struggling to maintain control, shouted, "Crows! Be careful!"

The car crashed into a tree. Vijay, Anuj, and Jessica, though dazed, quickly recovered.

Anuj, urgent, said, "We need to finish this."

Jessica, focused, added, "Grab everything. We can't delay."

They exited the car, carrying the cursed gold and the idol, and made their way towards the waterfall. The sky deepened in red, and acid rain began to fall.

Vijay, shouting over the rain, directed, "This is the place! Hurry!"

The crows circled above as the scene abruptly faded.

Inside the Sayal Temple, Vijay, Jessica, and Anuj navigated through the waterfall and secret tunnels. They encountered a three-headed wolf, a creature familiar from their dreams.

Anuj, astonished, exclaimed, "This is the same wolf from our dreams!"

Vijay, readying for a fight, instructed, "Be prepared, it will attack!"

The wolf attacked Anuj and Vijay, but retreated in fear upon seeing Jessica. Yakshini then appeared.

Yakshini, infuriated, demanded, "How dare you come here!"

Yakshini unleashed her divine powers. Jessica, standing firm, frightened Yakshini. Their faces bore a striking resemblance.

Yakshini, in shock, asked, "You... You are Durgavati?"

Jessica, though injured, found strength. She seized a sword and struck Yakshini, wounding her. The wolf was also slain.

Jessica, shouting triumphantly, declared, "This is your end, Yakshini!"

She destroyed Yakshini's idol and burned the cursed gold. Yakshini screamed as her body combusted and turned to ashes.

Yakshini, *in her final moments, screamed, "I will return!"*

In the hospital, calm had been restored. Vijay's wife's surgery was successful. Jessica and Anuj visited her.

Jessica, *answering her phone, responded, "What? Grandfather is dead? (sadly) Now I am free from Yakshini's curse..."*

Jessica felt a bittersweet mix of sorrow and relief, knowing her grandfather was freed from Yakshini's immortality curse. Tears filled her eyes as she found solace for her grandfather.

●

Jessica pondered aloud, "Why did Yakshini's face resemble mine? And where did this power come from?"

Suddenly, Acharya's voice echoed in the corridor.

Acharya

"I can answer that..."

Jessica was startled to see Acharya.

Acharya

"Do you not understand why I was pursuing you?"

The scene shifted to a hilltop where Acharya and Jessica stood.

Acharya

"These ruins belong to your ancestors, Jessica. You are not Robertson's granddaughter; you are the last heir of the Sayal royal family. You are the reincarnation of Queen Durgavati."

Jessica was stunned. Acharya unveiled the truth.

Acharya

"At the airport, I didn't send my men to kidnap you to kill you but to ensure you married Imad. Dinesh was killed by Imad, not by me. Our ancestors have safeguarded you for years."

Outside the ruined temple, Imad, holding Yakshini's bracelet, stood in silence.

Imad

(calling out)

"Yakshini!"

A figure appeared behind him—it was Yakshini.

Yakshini

"The ages have changed, but human greed remains unchanged."

The screen faded to black, suggesting Yakshini's return and the continuation of the story.

Imad's Secret Alliance

The cold mountain wind howled through the dense forest as Imad navigated the treacherous path. His horse's hooves clattered on the rocky trail, the rhythmic sound echoing in the stillness of the night. The moon, barely a sliver in the sky, cast elongated shadows that seemed to shift and writhe with every gust of wind. Imad's dark cloak billowed behind him, its edges flapping like dark wings in the gusty air.

He reached a concealed entrance, obscured by the constant rush of a cascading waterfall. Imad dismounted with practiced ease, his heavy boots splashing in the shallow pool beneath the falls. He approached the rock face, which appeared as solid and unyielding as the mountains surrounding it. His gloved hand found the hidden lever expertly camouflaged within the stone. With a firm tug, the rock face shifted and groaned, revealing a narrow, dark passageway that spiraled downward.

As Imad descended the winding stairs, the temperature dropped noticeably. The air grew damp and musty, and the only sound was the distant, echoing drip of water from the cavern ceiling. The staircase eventually opened into an expansive underground hall. Imad's eyes adjusted to the dim light emanating from flickering torches that cast dancing shadows on the cavern walls.

The hall was a hive of activity. A sense of disciplined chaos filled the air as the secret army prepared for their long-awaited retribution. Men and women moved with a purpose, their faces marked by grim determination. Blacksmiths worked at a blistering pace, hammering out intricate designs on swords and armor, the sparks flying with each strike. The clang of metal on metal was a constant backdrop, a rhythmic reminder of the preparation for the impending conflict.

Imad navigated through the bustling hall, his presence commanding immediate respect. He reached the command chamber, a grand space adorned with ancient tapestries and illuminated by the soft, golden glow of countless candles. The room was dominated by a massive, ornate table covered with detailed maps and charts. The walls were lined with historical relics and trophies, each telling the story of past victories and defeats.

Around the table stood a group of elderly figures, their robes rich with the symbols of ancient power. Their faces were lined with age and experience, their eyes sharp and discerning.

These were the custodians of a centuries-old secret, the leaders of the hidden faction that had awaited this moment for generations.

Imad approached the head of the table, where an elder with a long white beard and piercing eyes stood. The elder's gaze met Imad's with a mixture of respect and expectation.

"Imad," the elder intoned, his voice echoing with the weight of history. "You have returned. The time has come for us to reclaim our lost honor."

Imad nodded, his expression resolute. "Yes, the time has come. Our ancestors' defeat must be avenged. With Yakshini's last remaining bracelet, we will rise again and reclaim what was taken from us."

The elder's eyes gleamed with approval as he gestured towards a hidden alcove. There, resting on an elaborately carved pedestal, was an ancient artifact—a golden scepter, encrusted with mystical runes that seemed to pulsate with a soft, eerie glow.

"This scepter," the elder explained with reverence, "holds the power to awaken the spirit of Yakshini. Once activated, it will summon the strength of our forebears and empower us to avenge our ancestors' defeat."

Imad approached the scepter with a sense of awe and responsibility. He lifted it carefully, feeling the weight of both the artifact and the task before him. The scepter's surface was cool to the touch, its glow a faint reminder of the mystical forces it harbored.

As Imad prepared to leave, the scene transitioned to a sweeping view of the hidden valley where the army was drilling. The valley was a well-concealed stronghold, surrounded by ancient fortifications and camouflaged bunkers. The soldiers, clad in traditional Afghan warrior *attire, moved with practiced precision, their banners fluttering in the dim light. The entire area was alive with the sound of preparation—horse hooves, the clanging of weapons, and the murmur of voices filled the air.*

Montages flashed through Imad's mind, each one a vivid memory of the past:

***Jessica as Durgavati**: Scenes of Jessica in her previous incarnation as the warrior princess Durgavati. She stood tall and proud on the battlefield, her armor gleaming as she led her troops with unwavering courage. The battles were fierce, her enemies falling before her as she wielded her sword with unparalleled skill.*

***The Afghan Army's Defeat**: A series of battle scenes depicting the Afghan army's defeat at the hands of Yakshini's mystical forces. The soldiers fought bravely but were ultimately overwhelmed by the supernatural strength of Yakshini and her minions. The final moments of the battle showed the despair and heartbreak of the Afghan warriors as they fell one by one.*

3. **Imad's Legacy**: Scenes of Imad's ancestors, their faces etched with solemn determination as they vowed revenge. Young Imad trained with a fierce dedication, honing his skills and preparing for the day when they would rise again. The legacy of his lineage was a powerful reminder of the long-standing feud and the quest for retribution.

Returning to the command chamber, Imad found the elder waiting with a ceremonial dagger. The blade gleamed with an ethereal light, its surface etched with ancient symbols that pulsed with a soft glow.

"With this dagger," the elder said solemnly, "you will invoke the spirit of our ancestors. The time for our revenge draws near, and with Yakshini's power, we will reclaim our honor."

Imad accepted the dagger with reverence, placing it beside the scepter. The weight of the artifact and the dagger symbolized the heavy burden of his mission. The scene pulled back to *reveal the entire base, alive with activity and anticipation. The atmosphere was thick with the sense of impending conflict, the soldiers' preparation a testament to the seriousness of their cause.*

As Imad exited the base, the sky above the hidden valley was shrouded in a tempestuous darkness. The storm clouds gathered, crackling with lightning and thunder. Imad stood on a cliff, overlooking the valley, his face set in a mask of determination. The storm seemed to reflect the turmoil and the epic struggle that was about to unfold.

The camera panned out, capturing the ominous sky and the bustling preparations below. The scene ended with a sense of foreboding, setting the stage for the next chapter in the epic saga.

The scene faded, leaving behind the weight of ancient vengeance and the promise of a new era of conflict.

TO BE CONTINUED...

Post Credit Scene

Jessica, now embracing her identity as Durgavati's reincarnation, prepares for new challenges. Imad, with Yakshini's bracelet, plots to resurrect her. The ancient struggle between good and evil is far from over...

Legend speaks of Princess Durgawati, a name revered as much for its beauty as for its power. Her birth was no ordinary event; it is said that the gods themselves blessed her parents, who had long prayed for a child. The heavens opened up in response to their prayers, and thus was born Durgawati—a princess whose very existence was seen as a divine gift. From the moment she took her first breath, the kingdom knew she was destined for greatness.

As she grew older, it became clear that Durgawati was no ordinary princess. Her beauty was unparalleled, with eyes that shone like the brightest stars and a grace that left all who saw her in awe. But it was not just her beauty that made her special—it was her strength. In battle, she was as fierce as any warrior, unmatched in the arts of archery and swordsmanship. Many said that watching her fight was like witnessing the goddess Durga herself descend to the battlefield, her movements so swift and precise that enemies trembled at the mere mention of her name.

Her fame spread far and wide, and kingdoms across the land spoke of her as the "Warrior Princess." She could strike down an enemy from hundreds of yards away with her bow, and her skill with the sword was so legendary that even the greatest knights and warriors bowed to her talent. It was not long before tales of her exploits reached distant lands, and many sought her hand in marriage, hoping to win the heart of the powerful princess. But Durgawati had no interest in these suitors. She was devoted to her people, her kingdom, and her duty. Her focus was on protecting her land from the invaders and ensuring peace, not on personal glory or love.

However, despite her many victories and the devotion of her people, an air of mystery always surrounded Princess Durgawati. She was a woman of few words, and while she was beloved by all, very little was known about her personal life. Even her closest aides could not fully understand the depths of her thoughts or emotions. And then, one fateful day, she vanished—without a trace.

It was as if she had disappeared into thin air. There were no signs of struggle, no witnesses to her departure. One moment she was there, leading her kingdom with the same bravery and wisdom she had always shown, and the next, she was gone. Her people searched far and wide, sending out armies, scouts, and scholars to find any clue as to what might have happened. Rumors began to swirl: some believed she had been taken by the gods, a reward for her divine lineage and unmatched virtue. Others whispered of a forbidden love that had driven her to abandon her duties. Still, others spoke of darker forces, of ancient curses and forgotten enemies who had long harbored a grudge against her.

As the years passed, the mystery only deepened. There were stories of sightings—glimpses of a woman matching Durgawati's description seen in distant lands, leading secret rebellions or wandering the forests in solitude. Some claimed to have heard her voice in the wind, calling out from beyond the veil of time. But every lead, every clue, eventually turned cold. The princess, once so powerful and beloved, had simply vanished.

But why? What truly happened to Princess Durgawati on that fateful day? What secret was so great that it led to her sudden disappearance, one that no one has been able to uncover even after centuries of searching? Was it the gods who took her, or was there something far more earthly, far more sinister, at play?

For hundreds of years, historians, warriors, and treasure hunters alike have sought the truth, each one hoping to be the first to solve the riddle of her disappearance. And yet, the secret remains buried, locked away in the shadows of time, leaving the world to wonder: Was she a mere mortal, or was she something more—something too powerful, too dangerous for the world to hold onto?

The question lingers like a haunting whisper in the wind. The secret of Princess Durgawati's fate remains untold. But the search for the truth continues, with the hope that one day, the world will finally learn the answer to the greatest mystery it has ever known...

Coming Soon: Yakshini 2 - Adhura Itihaas

• 169 •

The END

Written By Rahul Chatterjee

Author's Letter

Dear Readers,

I am Rahul Chatterjee, a filmmaker and editor by profession, and it is with great pride and passion that I present to you Yakshini. India is a land steeped in history, culture, and mythology, where every stone has a story and every breeze carries a whisper of the past. This book is a humble attempt to bring to light some of the deep-rooted legends and mystical tales that are woven into the very fabric of our nation.

The inspiration for Yakshini comes from my deep admiration for India's rich cultural heritage. Our country is home to countless stories—stories of gods and demons, of love and betrayal, of sacrifice and valor. These tales are not just folklore; they are a part of who we are, shaping our beliefs and our identity. I believe that these stories deserve to be told and shared with the world, not just as relics of the past but as living, breathing narratives that continue to influence us today.

Before this, I wrote Samaykaal, a novel that explored the concept of time travel while paying tribute to our great Sanatan Dharma. Through Samaykaal, I aimed to delve into the timeless principles that have guided our civilization for millennia. With Yakshini, I wanted to explore a different aspect of our culture—the mystical and the supernatural, the hidden forces that have always been a part of our land.

But as you reach the end of this book, let me assure you, this is not the end of the story. What you have just read is only the beginning—a prelude to a much larger saga. The chaos that has been unleashed is far from over. In fact, it is just beginning. The forces that have been awakened will bring about a reckoning, a doomsday of sorts, where the fate of many will hang in the balance.

So, as you close this book, remember that the story of Yakshini is not finished. It is the dawn of a new era, where ancient powers clash with modern ambitions, where the lines between good and evil blur, and where the true nature of the forces that shape our world will be revealed.

Thank you for joining me on this journey. The road ahead is fraught with danger, but also with discovery. I hope you will walk it with me, as the saga continues.

With warm regards,

Rahul Chatterjee

Filmmaker and Author